New Year Newish Me

We Are All Work In Progress

Macy Milldale

Cover design by: James at Goonwrite.com

I dedicate this book to my mother Eleanor...I wish I had known you more...

I also dedicate it to my husband and daughter and remind them of what they mean to me.

Finally to mental health staff everywhere.. we do make a difference.

xxx

Contents

Acknowledgements

I would like to thank the Centre For Clinical Interventions Website for allowing me to utilise their workbook information in this story.

I have been using their CBT techniques for years in my job as a mental health nurse.
Their website is free to use and covers many mental health topics. The workbooks are written in straightforward language.

I would like to thank most heartedly Rosemary Blake for helping me bring this book to market and my other bestie Cerys Linton. Both of these are writers in their own name so please look them up on Amazon.

I would also like to thank my fellow writers in the Coalville Writers Group who have all at some point read and advised me on my story, especially Peter Huckerby and Douglas GIlmour, again check out their work on Amazon.

Chapter 1

'How do I look in this?' Claire tottered around the changing room, striking different poses as if on the catwalk.

Dee smiled wryly at her friend's daring exhibition in front of the teenage girls in the communal area.

'Go on Dee, go get that little red number to try on. I know you think it will clash with your hair, but it won't. Try something different for a change other than black.'

Not wanting to disappoint her friend, Dee launched herself back into the hell hole of a shop that was known to cater for adolescents. She wandered aimlessly unable to remember where the dress was. She would try it on to amuse her friend but had no intention of buying it.

The jangle of the music and the brightness of the lights made her feel a little light -headed. She wasn't feeling the spirit of the annual Christmas party dress hunt.

Dee was distracted by the snippets of conversations she heard while scanning the aisles. She was bemused by girls taking selfies and sending photos of the items they were considering buying. Then they stood waiting for snapchat approval from besties. She wished that, at thirty -five, her only worry was whether to go vampy or geeky.

A scarlet dress glittering in the corner called to her. Dee stood transfixed, dreaming of having the kind of figure that would show it off. It was designed for a waif with pert breasts. It had sequins and so it would be a disaster to wash. She needed to think practically. She grabbed it as if it were a lifejacket under a plane seat and scurried off to the changing room.

She reluctantly unzipped her jeans and pulled off her jumper. The cubicle was cold and the lighting was so unflattering. If she could just breath in a little more, she could ease it over her hips without splitting the seams. Alas, the zip at the back just would not do up. She stopped the contortionist act. '*Now my mascara has run and I look like Alice Cooper,*' she didn't know whether to laugh or cry.

Claire was trying on a bodycon for her winter getaway. She looked at her shapely, toned body in the mirror. She tried to avoid looking at her thighs but, in the end, had to admit 'damn I'll need to wear a long skirt.' She ripped the dress off and slung it at the hanger.

'How're you getting on with that dress Dee?'

'No good, I couldn't get it on.'

'Are you sure?'

'Come and see if you don't believe me.'

Claire ripped open Dee's curtain and looked her friend up and down.'Come on let's go for a coffee. I'm sure you will find something online.'

They walked arm in arm, the same way they had since they first met at nursing college. There was not long as it was nearly closing time at the shopping centre. People were scuttling by, rushing to catch the bus and to get home for hot tea after a stressful evening of Christmas shopping. Everyone was laden with bags of toiletries and other items that would end up in tombola raffles later in the year. The aroma of the coffee shop beckoned, it felt like a welcome retreat.

'There you go, lemon drizzle.' Claire knew cake always cheered her friend up.

'Will you have half with me?' Dee knew that Claire would always refuse.

'Come on then Dee. New Year and all that, are you going to look for another job?'

'Yeah and get a new man and lose half my body weight.' She said this in between coping with mouthfuls of a particularly dry slice of cake.

'What about you then Claire? You said you wanted to travel more and take up yoga.'

'I never plan anything you know that.' She was a little distracted by a business type with a sharp beard, who was scrolling on his phone.

'Are you ready for another relationship do you think? It's been a while and you said you were fed up with being on your own.'

'Maybe, if not I might go to the Amazon and study the wildlife. Hopefully, there'll be some Tom Hardy look-alike working there as an anthropologist.' She giggled and then suggested it was time for them to go.

Dee drove home. The rain pounded down and the glare from headlights made her eyes feel heavy. She hoped her mum was still up, ready to make her a hot chocolate and to have a chat or maybe watch some television.

Dee thought about her life. She wondered if she would ever feel completely happy.

Was it possible to have a life like those in the TV realities shows 'The Housewives of Timbuktu?' Surely it was all made up and anyway she wouldn't want to just party all day. She also disliked false nails. She remembered how she had once paid forty pounds for a set before going on holiday, she lost one doing her suitcase zip up and a further one somewhere on the plane. It had worried her immensely. She never tracked it down and wondered if it had ended up in someone's microwaved dinner.

The stupid satnav, for some reason when she was tired, or it was dark, all the roads looked different and now she was heading in the wrong direction on the motorway. She started to think about the self-esteem group and what she wanted to change in the New Year and how she'd do it. At fourteen stones, she knew she needed to lose weight, not just for her body image but also her health. She pictured her body. She had nurse's legs, heavy and blighted by varicose veins. She had nurse's arms, muscular but thick. Somehow or other she had ended up, though, with a sumo wrestler stomach and bum, which was of course nothing to do with nursing. She reminded herself she had not watched Embarrassing Bodies on catch-up yet. She felt down in the glove compartment. How lucky it was that a chocolate Twirl was still left over from the multi-pack. She was feeling a little hungry.

Dee's mum was still up but her dad had gone for his Friday drink. She was watching a recorded episode of 'Vera' but paused it to speak to her daughter.

'Shall I do us a drink love?'

Dee slumped in the armchair nearest the fire. She looked up at the bookshelf and her school photo when she was four. It had taken pride of place up there since she had started school, alongside a photo of her when she had qualified as a nurse. Claire was also in the photo as Dee's mum had felt sorry that Claire's own mum hadn't attended the graduation ceremony.

'Do you want a bit of that cherry cake from yesterday love?' her mum shouted from the kitchen. So how was our Claire then?'

'Still spending too much money on clothes and avoiding having a relationship. Other than that, okay.'

'I don't understand her. Looking how she does, working as a matron and owning her own house. You think she would want a child by now.'

Dee shot a glance at her mum. Her mum noticed it and avoided eye contact.

'I don't think Claire's interested in being a mother. What you're really trying to say is that I should have a home and family.' Dee gazed at the dying embers of the fire.

'It wasn't a dig at you love. You've just got to be careful who you fall for next time.'

'Well, we thought that Martin was decent to start with.'

'He was just obsessed with that son of his. Was it three times a week he was taking him to rugby? He never made any time for you.'

'I know and then there was Luke before him. If only he had carried on with his gambling counselling, we may have made it work.'

'This year you will meet someone Dee, you can't be unlucky forever.'

'Yeah, maybe Mum.'

After eating the cake, Dee was struggling to keep her eyes open and so she retired to her bedroom. Good old mum, she had put a hot water bottle in her bed. Dee snuggled deep under the duvet. The last thought she had before nodding off, was a reminder to buy a lotto ticket as it was a roll-over and she could change so many people's lives with it. She could pay for a psychologist for Claire to see why she was afraid of relationships. Then she could treat herself to an elephant sanctuary as well as a thatched cottage with a climbing rose up the side. She then started to worry about how she could accommodate an elephant sanctuary in the Lake District. Perhaps she could just fund one in Africa and have a webcam instead?

Meanwhile at Claire's house, she was tossing and turning as usual. She grabbed a magazine and flicked through the pages irritably. Perhaps she ought to consider trying a relationship? She thought that she would go to the self-esteem group with Dee, just to support her. She wouldn't get any benefit from it herself. The curtains were allowing a sliver of light through and there on the bedside table was the knife.

Chapter 2

Melissa struggled to get up in the night to take her three-year old to the toilet. It was so cold, and she was barely awake but managed to tumble the sleepy child onto the toilet and, mission accomplished, went back to bed. She caught a glimpse of Geoff snoring beside her and wondered how easy it would be to take the pillow and place it over his mouth, pressing down until the breathing stopped. For a moment she was tempted and then the rational side of her kicked in. She slid back down under the covers and looked at the alarm clock.

She thought about seeing Dee the next morning and smiled. If only her life could be more straightforward like Dee's. She lay awake trying to fantasise about a life without Geoff, desperately trying to conjure up an image of herself carefree and laughing. She thought about her schooldays and how she used to laugh a lot. She and Dee would go shopping and stalk some sixth former around the precinct. They would buy a doughnut each and munch on it while walking round the clothes shops. She smiled thinking about how many dresses she had touched with sticky fingers. Then the memories switched to her parents sitting her down at the age of thirteen and accusing her of ruining their marriage, of being demanding and different to the other kids. They asked her why she couldn't try harder to be the same as them and not so naughty? She felt a pang of bitterness followed by smugness when she recalled that a year later, she was diagnosed with attention deficit disorder. That made them feel guilty.

She rolled over and turned to face Geoff. How good it had been to start with. He had always been so loving and giving. How could things have come to this? What was the answer? She thought about what Geoff had been through at work. He had started to drink to cope. She could see that it would be easy to turn to drink,but not the other. . .

Tears began to trickle down her face, she sucked on her arm to stop them; afraid to wake Geoff up and stir an angry reaction.

Dee was always happy to see her even when Melissa had her two live-wire kids with her. Josh who was three and Tilly was nearly two. It would be great to see Dee on her own sometimes, but Geoff was always either stuck at work or needing to catch up with paperwork at weekends. It was well over a year since they had last had 'girlie' time. It was hard talking in the middle of a ball pit; Melissa was distractible enough without crawling around and entertaining the kids at the same time.

Dee looked at Melissa, she had always felt so jealous of her. She had what she thought was a perfect marriage, two adorable kids and a beautiful home. Dee wanted the same but had just given up hope of it ever happening. She could not get over that Melissa had ended up so much better off than her. As a teenager Melissa had smoked cannabis and slept around. She was always being sent home from school on report. Until she met Geoff, she was a nightmare. He had turned her around, if only Dee had someone like him....

In between games and romping around like a toddler herself, Dee told Melissa about the shopping trip with Claire.

'I am trying to convince her to come to this self-esteem group that's starting in February. I thought we could support each other. Are you sure you don't want to come as well? I know you still worry about not being a good enough mum and what people think of you. The yummy mummy brigade and that.'

'No, I can't come now, no time and Geoff never knows what time he will be in at night. Since the investigation, he has stayed late to check he has written everything in the records; you know, reporting exactly what was said and all that. I don't get any time to myself.'

'Poor Geoff, he couldn't have foreseen that the woman would just flip in the middle of the night and kill herself and the baby. He shouldn't keep dwelling on it, should he?'

'Do you want a coffee, Dee?'

The women chatted about the kids and their plans

for the year ahead. Melissa had no plans really, perhaps a caravan holiday in the spring and to decorate the kitchen. She wanted to get back to work part time. She was a trained teaching assistant and missed her work, but the childcare costs were daylight robbery, so it made sense for her to wait till Josh started school.

'Well, I want to meet Mr. Right this year and go for promotion, and of course as usual I want to lose weight,' Dee said before taking a mouthful of deluxe hot chocolate with marshmallows.

'Yeah, you deserve a good year, Dee. You've had your share of losers and you should be a ward manager by now. You have been a nurse since you were twenty-one. I don't know though whether you will like it? You don't like people not liking you do you and I guess when you're the boss that's what will happen?'

'Well, I won't have to take things personally. I should be more like Claire and toughen up. As long as I am fair and still prepared to roll my sleeves up; I don't see why people would dislike me. I know what you mean though, but I guess there is only one way to find out. How, though, am I going to meet a decent bloke?'

'You've tried all the dating sites now, other than the dodgy ones. So how about a further education course or a conservation club, or animal sanctuary work; try to meet a volunteer?'

'I hadn't thought about volunteering but it's not a bad idea, I guess. Well, I better get going as I am on a late today.' The two friends hugged, and Melissa watched from the window as Dee zoomed off in her red Mini.

Melissa sat for a moment thinking about her life. She longed to talk to Dee, to tell her how miserable she was and how desperate she was beginning to feel. She sat thinking about what the vicar had told her to do, either go to Relate or contact United Against Violence and Abuse. She would always say she would think about it and then she would avoid speaking to him again for the next few visits or sometimes avoid going at all. She knew Geoff would not go to Relate, he never said he was sorry and blamed her for driving him to get angry. As for United Against Violence and Abuse they would probably encourage her to leave him. It felt too much of a big decision. He was so unhappy and stressed it was not his fault' he just lost it sometimes. He would change, she was sure of it. If he didn't perhaps she would need to change and provide a more relaxed atmosphere for him to come home to. That was it, she would get prepared even earlier at night for his return; then tea would be on the table when he got home. Then, if she could stop the kids sleeping in the daytime, they would be tired for bed earlier and this would give them more adult time. Maybe the romance would come back? Eager to get home and try out her new plan, she scooped up the kids and loaded them into her estate car. For once Melissa felt positive.

Chapter 3

Dee's late shift was tiring. More and more admissions for chest infections and pneumonia and no beds.

Irritable relatives demanding to know what support the patient would get when they were discharged. Student nurses asking questions: why and what. Junior nurses feigning migraines to leave early so that they could go clubbing. Dee's head was throbbing when she left and stepped out into the chilly, black night. While standing de-icing her car, she remembered the days she would leave a late shift and go dancing with Claire and some junior doctor and then get up at five for the early shift. Now she just longed for a soak in the bath and Facebook, or possibly a catch up on Holby City. Was this going to be her life from now on? Was she doomed to be a spinster? A modern-day Florence Nightingale. She laughed reminding herself that Flo did have a few perks of the job.

Driving home she thought about her life and compared it to other people's. She always tried to piece together the reason she had missed the opportunity to meet the right fella. She had had many chances, but all fizzled into nothing for various reasons. They were either married to their work, so the timing was wrong; or just wanted a casual affair because they had come out of a nasty divorce. She had had her share of toxic relationships, womanisers, gamblers, drinkers; all with one thing in common - they were all emotionally unavailable.

Dee had taken an emotional battering before she had left them, or they had rejected her. She would move to the next loser she thought she could fix, typical behaviour of a nurse and everything. Ever the rescuer and ever naïve. She would often minimize their destructive behavior by blaming it on herself. If only she was thinner, more attractive; did not work shifts. The last candidate appeared hopeful. She had met him a year ago, after his mother had been admitted to the ward. The positives were that he had been divorced for two years so he was over the playing the field urge and the 'woe is me' stage, but he was a devoted dad to son Toby. So besotted that it was hard to squeeze Dee into a schedule of rugby training,, son and dad time and his work. After six months of realising that Martin was only interested in a part time relationship and keeping their relationship separate from his son, Dee had called it quits. She wanted to be a part of a unit fulltime, not a timeshare. She wanted a family and to make a family. It was plain to see Martin already had his family.

Dee was still waiting for her Jane Austen romance. The one where she is pursued by a man in a frilly white shirt- emerging wet from a lake; she had always thought the series of Pride and Prejudice better than the film for this reason. She was waiting for her chick-flick ending.

In the week to come she put some thought to the voluntary work idea and she decided to go and visit the local National Trust property to discuss becoming a conservation volunteer. She had arranged to visit and have a chat with a warden called Tom. All in all, she thought it was worth a shot at networking and even if Mr. Darcy was not there; she might meet some new and interesting people.

She knew she was no catch though. She could only bank her hopes on some divorced man with a ready-made family. She predicted that no one would want a baby with her. It would therefore be handy to find a widower with a young baby to nurture, but she guessed that would be hard to find. It was not as though they were advertised on Gumtree. She had always felt humbled by any offers of a romance as she never felt worthy. She went into relationships with no expectations, no sense of her own needs, just an assumption that it would all end up badly.

Perhaps there would be an interesting man at the conservation club? She needed to be there for nine on Sunday morning and she just hoped it would not be raining as she had no truly waterproof mascara.

Seven o' clock Sunday morning, she looked through her curtains. Thick fog and very, very cold. She wondered how many layers of the newly purchased clothes from a famous outdoor shop she should wear. Thermal tights or socks, perhaps both. She treated herself to a cup of tea and three ginger nuts to dunk, well it was Sunday. She was glad she had three as it reminded her that really it was already mid-January and the diet should have started at the beginning of the year. She needed to get onto it, but best leave it for this week there were inspections at work so it would be stressful.

Her mum was up early to make her a flask and a cheese and pickle cob for break time. Her dad had offered to drive her as the weather was bad, but she declined. He had however nipped out and turned her engine on to warm the car, checked her tyres were alright and filled the screen wash up. It was a half hour drive to The Grange. She had been around the grounds several times a year but had never been inside, mainly due to the cost. Anyway once you had seen one of those places; they kind of all looked the same. She drove extremely tentatively relying on the sat nav and arrived half an hour early. She checked her mascara was still intact, but she was struggling to breathe with all the clobber on. She waited, listening to her favourite music, as she saw other cars begin to pull up in the car park. Various shades of grey hairstyles began to disembark and walk in. Lots of couples and single women. Damn she wasn't the only one with the same idea. Serves her right, she should be doing it to preserve heritage; not to meet a husband. She thought for a moment of staying in the car and just driving off. She could claim that a pressing matter had arisen but she that she would come in the spring. On the other hand, they may be relying on her and so feeling guilty she stumbled stiffly out of the car as she couldn't bend her knees in the thermal tights without intense pain.

There were several newbies joining the group. The warden introduced himself as Tom and gave an overview of what opportunities were available to partake in and a season-by-season breakdown of works planned. So much to do, but other than taking parties around to see the lambing, nothing particularly appealed to her. Everything involved bending.

Tom turned to Dee and asked with a relaxed and confident air. 'Is there anything that takes your fancy?' Funnily enough she was scanning the room for any potential candidates when she realized, he was asking her about activities.

'The lambing and maybe the dry-stone walling, if I can bend and kneel enough to do it.'

'Great, we rely on volunteers and it's good that so many of you have come forward. I'll show you all round the house and gardens now, please follow me.'

It seemed that Tom was the only eligible man in the room, other than Bill who she suspected could be in his early sixties. There were at least four couples and two-family units there, as well as numerous single women one of whom, Kate, attached herself to Dee and they chatted idly as Tom showed them around the building and grounds. The Grange was a huge place, but still felt like a home. She imagined women with long gowns bustling around the rooms, horses and carriages thundering up the driveway. She had walked the grounds many times but noticed anew that as the fog lifted and the sun began to trickle through, the light danced with silhouettes of trees. Dee half expected to see a fairy in the midst of them. It was a magical place. She observed how Tom answered everyone's queries with light-hearted banter and interest. He made people feel welcome and was full of boundless facts, incidental tales about the place and gossip about how the other half lived. She observed him to be probably about mid- forties, no wedding ring and ruddy faced but then it was cold. He was sort of rugby player built and like her needed to stop eating crusty cobs. That reminded her it must be break time by now.

It is difficult eating crusty things when having a conversation. She made a mental note to just bring a Twix next time. Kate was looking to make new friends after moving to the area for a job. She did however have a partner and therefore was not a threat to Dee's plans to meet someone. By eleven-thirty they all left, agreeing when they would commit to coming again. Dee would go the following Saturday for a litter pick, deep joy. She liked Kate though and felt sorry that she didn't know anyone else, so she would come for her sake. Dee liked to help others, a good attribute if you are a nurse.

She had phoned ahead to tell her parents she was on the way back, so her mum had run her a bath, even put crystals in it and put her dressing gown and slippers by the fire to warm. There was a cup of tea waiting and a small slice of madeira cake just until lunch, after all it would not be ready for another half an hour.

Over lunch she told her parents all about her morning and Kate and Tom's enthusiasm. In fact, she was surprised how much there was to say about Tom. Her mum who was always eager to see her daughter with a potential National Trust warden remarked.

'Tom must live a wonderful life, working in such surroundings; you know, with wildlife and things. I bet he gets a cottage on site so he can keep an eye on the place. Can you imagine how nice that would be, waking up and walking in the woodland before the gates are open to the rest of us? Are you ready for apple pie now love, do you want custard or cream?'

Dee stared out of the window after lunch, her dad was snoozing and her mum reading the paper. Dee sat thinking about how she had always wanted a thatched cottage with a rose growing up the side in a village opposite a green, where people just call in for a coffee on a whim; without having to text first. She would have a big wooden table and one of those open fires. She would be on the village fete committee and she and her mum would sell fresh cream scones. Outside, rain began to pour. As she turned away to wash up, she missed the rainbow starting to form in the distance.

Chapter 4

Monday morning was always a nightmare for Matron Claire. Catching up on the weekend reports on deaths and staff errors. Today would be a tricky one as she had a report of a junior nurse who had administered the wrong dose of analgesic. The nurse had realised and done it afterwards and had admitted it to the medics. Luckily, the patient had just slept rather heavily. The relatives had been informed and were understanding when the nurse had apologized.

'Come in Beth,' she made her voice stern as the young newly-qualified nurse entered her office. What Claire wanted to say was not what came out of her mouth. What she found herself saying were her own mother's words.

'There might not be a next time Beth, if you are stressed take a break but this is the job; you need to be more resilient.'

The young girl left feeling shaken and unvalued, doubting her ability to continue the job but also resentful at the understaffed ward and the pressures put upon her.

'Rotten cow,' she mumbled under her breath and then vowed to look at job adverts that day.

Claire sat pondering what she had said. She had wanted to say some positives about the girl and just to advise her to learn from her mistakes. She had wanted to be supportive. She had wanted to let her hear what she herself had needed to hear as a child, that she was good enough and valued. That her mother believed her, that it was John coming onto her and not the other way. She visualized her mum saying it would be best if Claire could stay with her gran for the night while her mum absorbed what Claire had told her about John. She said it was just to give everyone some space. She didn't mind going to gran's, knowing her mum would get rid of John and that she would be back home the next day. It was not to be. So, from the age of fourteen Claire lived with her gran and her mum lived with John. Claire's mum was convinced her daughter had been flirting with John and didn't believe that her boyfriend was a paedophile.

Whenever Dee and Claire could they met in the staff canteen for lunch. One of them was nearly always late or sometimes could not make it at all due to medical emergencies or urgent meetings. Today though they had managed half an hour.

'I want you to take over as manager on Ward 17 when Mandy goes for maternity leave in March. She's having the full year off she's decided.' Claire looked at Dee in an assertive manner across the table.

'Me? I don't work on Ward 17 and doesn't anyone else want to do it?' Dee was shocked by the proposal.

'I want you to do it. You know there's poor morale on

the ward and you will be right for the job; steady it all down and show some positivity.'

'I don't know Claire; I'll think about it but thanks for asking me.'

'Dee for goodness sake, you've been saying for ages you want a go at being a ward manager, here's your chance; stop doubting yourself.' Claire hated weaknesses in others, it reminded her of her own.

'I'm just worried that the staff don't know me and won't respect me when I ask them to do something. There's been some bitchiness on there hasn't there and it's cliquey. I might wait till something comes up on my own ward.'

Claire frowned, 'That's it, talk yourself down like you always do, men, jobs, red dresses.' Seeing Dee bow her head Claire realized she had overstepped the mark and added; 'Dee I want you to try it, it's easier managing people you don't know. You'll be great.'

Dee wanted to ask if Claire had thought anymore about the self-esteem group. As if reading her mind, Claire announced she would go with her as her support rather than because she felt it would benefit herself. It would be every Tuesday starting the first of February for ten weeks. Next week was the first one.

Monday night was difficult for Dee. She sat thinking, as she had to let Claire know about the job by the end of the week. It was all she ever wanted, recognition, a sense of achievement and a chance to improve patient care and have a say in it. Her parents were encouraging her to take the job and her mum was instantly on the phone telling her best friend about her daughter being asked to be a Sister. Dee's mind was in turmoil. What if the staff did not respect her decisions or gossiped about her and what if they didn't ask her to parties and sent her to Coventry? It would just be like school again.

At primary school Dee had been the chubby one, with a brace and reading glasses. She always ended up tagging along in a group of four. Her 'so called' best friend Lucy, would swap and change her allegiance to her at the drop of a hat. Dee's mum would try to socially engineer and arrange sleep overs, roller skating, parties but still Dee was often left out. She would dread lunch, having to ask if it was okay to sit beside Lucy or did Lucy want to sit with Hannah that day. Often by the time she got to the table it was full and she would have to sit with the boys. It was always strange, as well, when others arranged sleepovers, they were only allowed so many people so could she come next time. Dee would go home telling her mum she felt left out, and Dee's mum would worry and cry and go to speak to the teachers and arrange more sleepovers. Just before starting secondary school that summer, Dee was determined to starve herself and only ate salad for a week. It made her ill and she got piles. She had her long hair professionally cut into a bob and her mum bought her a whole range of new clothes from the very shop she had seen the red dress. She felt okay about herself, more adult and ready for the change of school. The first day back though, her friends did not seem to notice her hair cut, or her new coat and shoes as they were more interested in making new friends. As the days went by, she would watch them from afar in the canteen laughing and fooling around with their new mates. That's when she noticed Melissa. She was alone too. No one would hang out with her as she was always mouthy and in trouble with the teachers for being loud and defiant. So, the two of them became friends. The ever so visible Melissa and the ever so invisible Dee.

Chapter 5

Dee had gone to the litter pick. She had managed without so much insulation and even managed to kneel. It was hard work though. Kate had joined her and the two worked as a team. Tom had been encouraging and continued with his light-hearted wit. Everyone appreciated it, especially since it was cold. Dee often caught herself trying to analyse him, trying to work out what kind of person he was and whether he could be attached. She thought he would probably be into skinny women who were super fit and outdoorsy. So, after a while she stopped trying to read him and even convinced herself he could maybe have a male partner at home, eagerly baking scones for the village fete.

It was a frosty Tuesday night when Claire and Dee drove way out of town for the self-esteem group. They went afar so as not to bump into work colleagues or even patients. Who wants to be managed by someone with low self-esteem or nursed by an unconfident person? They did not want anyone to know they had issues.

On arriving at the group, Dee was surprised at how many professional looking people were there: younger, older, glamorous and some still in business suits as if they had set off straight from work. Joy was the woman leading the session. She was a psychologist and a larger-than-life figure. She, of course, dressed for the part in an outfit that looked like she had been professionally colour-matched, to make sure the aura around her was positive. She had on a soft green jumper with a floaty, floral, scarf, navy trousers and navy pumps. Dee admired her presentation and decided she could book in for a personal shopper session; using her increased salary now she had tentatively decided to trial the Ward Manager's job.

Dee looked around the GP surgery's magnolia painted meeting room. It was totally bland with a couple of wonky pictures of sunflowers and one of a country cottage. The orange, vinyl seats, she supposed, were to give a bright appearance. She began to think what horrors doctors had to deal with. Most of her own patients were elderly, infirm people. She couldn't bear the thought of having to deal with ill children, or young adults with cancer. Who would be a GP? A ten-minute appointment to save someone, to impress someone, who had perhaps waited two weeks for that timeslot. No pressure there then. No wonder they all wanted to go to Australia to work. At least there, it would still be sunny when they got off work an hour or so late, she thought.

'Welcome all. I am Joy. You have all taken your first steps in learning about yourselves and who you want to be by attending today. We are going to be thinking now about what we mean by self-esteem. It is a phrase everyone uses but do we know what it means? Any ideas? I will write them on the flipchart,' Joy's boundless energy filled the whole void of the uninviting room.

Silence in the group, no one daring to make the first move and talk first. Dee felt impelled to help and blurted out awkwardly.

'Well, I think it's about feeling okay about yourself. Your personality and the way you look.'

'Good answer. It's not necessarily being at the stage where you feel great about yourself but 'okay' should be what we are aiming for, 'great' would be a bonus.' Joy wrote down what Dee said.

Other answers were added to the chart such as: 'feeling able to say no to people', 'not being too shy', 'being able to talk at a meeting'. 'not be put down by others'.

One of the group members barely looked up the whole time. Someone else had a stammer when they spoke. A young girl announced she was autistic and so struggled to even stay sitting in the group, but was doing it for her parents' sake. Someone else disclosed that they had been bullied at work and that was why they had lost confidence, but that they had been a high-flier up until that point.

Homework was to write down what people's aims for coming to the group were and to fill in a questionnaire to assess their self- esteem at the beginning of the group. At the end, another one would be completed to look for change. They were also to write a definition of what their self -esteem was like presently.

Claire sat with her head bowed most of the session

as if she were invisible, she was however deep in thought and she hated that. The urge to rush out the room, hide in the loo and cut with the contingency razor she had sneaked in her handbag became overwhelming and at the end of the session she dashed to the lavatory in relief. Dee, however, was prepared and followed Claire in. She stood outside the loo door and calmly told her friend to pass the offending item under the door to her.

'Dee go away, I need to do this.'

'Claire, talk to me instead, come on you did before.'

Claire opened the door and gave Dee the razor. She shut the door and threw up.

On the way home they discussed what their aims for the group were, and both concluded they just wanted to discover who they really were and learn strategies to make them feel okay about themselves.

'You see Dee, I'm not the person everyone thinks I am. I bet everyone thinks I am confident and full of myself. I've got to stop trying to get my mum to like me and notice me. I've got to give it up.'

'I think your mum probably doesn't like herself and because of that she finds it hard to give love to anyone else. Maybe she feels guilty for how she treated you and that is why she avoids you. I don't know, you'd think she'd want to make up for how she treated you in the past.' Dee offered.

'I just don't know what more I have to do in life to get

her to think well of me; to get her to love me,' the tears came again. She did not know why. She was thirty-five and a Matron. She had her own home, a wealthy admirer and several good friends. Why was she bothered what her mother thought of her? Claire felt angry with herself.

Claire would leave voicemails for her mother and it would take days for her to get back in touch. She would decline Claire's invitations and all conversations switched to her own worries rather than being a two-way effort. Claire resorted to 'liking' photos her mum posted on Facebook of her nights out with friends and her most recent new boyfriend. The old perpetrator had long gone. She stalked her mother wanting desperately to feel a part of her life but still her mum held her at arms-length like an old work acquaintance. Countless times she had broached her sadness over the lack of contact they had with each other, but her mother would deflect it by saying they both had busy lives. Each meeting would lead to a greater sense of rejection and bereavement over what should be and what should have been.

Claire turned to Dee, 'What do you think will make your life different Dee? Is it just about a more senior job and a new man?'

'Me, I would just like to feel a part of something and I want to feel liked by people.'

'But you are a part of something, your parents dote on you and you have Melissa and me.'

'Claire, I know, but my parents aren't always going

to be here, and I need to feel strong enough to manage without them bolstering me.'

Dee pulled up outside Claire's house. They agreed to meet the following week and in addition Claire agreed to look at a website on stopping self-harm.

Dee drove home thinking about how she hoped the course could help her, especially since she was starting her new job mid-March. She needed to be more assertive and emotionally stronger if she was going to be a manager. She thought about her earlier idea of booking in for a personal shopper experience, but then what was the point of buying new clothes as she would be losing weight soon. She sighed, it was Tuesday, and she was supposed to have started the diet again yesterday. Now she would have to wait till next week or maybe after starting the new job, as it would be stressful after all. Perhaps springtime would be the best opportunity to start dieting, when there would be more fresh salads in the shops? If she lost a few pounds a week, she could lose a couple of stones in total before August. She would then be a size twelve again. Then she could treat herself to new clothes. It all made perfect sense and she congratulated herself on the plan.

Dee's mum was waiting at home with tea and crumpets. She was worried Dee would be cold after such a long drive on a murky night. Dee told her mum everything about Joy and Claire and her plans for the personal shopper experience. They agreed to go together; it would be a reward for them both after Dee had accepted the job. Dee's dad raised his eyes from the newspaper and smiled at his girls. He hoped it would always be as it should; the three of them.

On going to bed, Dee noticed a text from earlier in the evening. It was from Kate at the volunteer group.

‘Hi Dee, having a house party Saturday evening. Would be great if you can come, being a last-minute idea. Let me know.’

Dee’s heart skipped a beat. She would not know anyone; she would be standing in the corner of the room on her own feeling awkward. Kate was a lot younger than her, so Kate’s friends probably would be too. No one would want an overweight ginger prude there. They would all be drinking shots and smoking pot. She was just about to text to decline the offer, due to work commitments when a second text arrived.

'Forgot to say, Tom's coming...'

Chapter 6

The lead up to Saturday night started on Friday night with Dee rooting through her wardrobe to see what she had to wear that was appropriate for a house party. Her mum sat on the bed to give opinions and Claire was on Facetime to offer moral support. She knew Kate lived in a small cottage and so she didn't need anything too pretentious. Was it enough to go for a woolly and jeans though? It could get a little stifling if they were going to be crammed into a galley kitchen? In the end the casting vote went to a pale pink lightweight jumper with navy jeans and suede ankle boots.

On the Saturday evening her mum helped her add light curls to her hair and helped do her makeup. Her mum was good at that. They put Abba on, and her mum even had a glass of fizz, as if she were getting ready for a night out as well. Dee, however, was still apprehensive and the nearer it got to going, the more she wanted to pull out. In fact, she could feel a bad headache coming on. It was no good going with a headache. As if sensing her daughter was looking for a get-out clause, her mum reached out and hugged her and told her how gorgeous she looked. She shouted for her husband to add support.

Dee stumbled in through Kate's front door looking apologetic that she had come. Kate as if sensing her new friend's awkwardness took her straight through to the kitchen and introduced Ben, her partner. Tom stood chatting to him. Ben then had to take a tray of nibbles around, leaving Tom and Dee alone.

'Hi Dee, how are you? You look lovely.'

'Oh, thanks Tom, how are you? It's a beautiful house, isn't it?'

'Yeah, it used to be the local baker's years ago. It's got so many old features, it's great.'

'I love old houses. They're just so expensive to buy, especially in a decent place. I love the feel of them though.'

'They take a lot of maintenance, but I think they're worth it. I have just inherited my family home and am trying to renovate it now. It's taking much longer than I thought it would, just doing it in my spare time.'

'Oh, I am sorry you have lost your parents Tom. How long ago was that?'

It turned out that Tom's mother had been involved in a fatal car accident in the previous year and his dad had died of cancer when Tom was a teenager. Just like Dee, he was an only child and just like Dee he had had a doting mother. The pair chatted away, oblivious to all going on around them, and declined karaoke and the other party activities that people always do when they are pie-eyed. Tom was really interested in Dee's job and the self-esteem group she was doing. Dee suddenly stopped to check if she was hogging him and boring him to death, but he must have felt fine about it as he didn't make an excuse to go and talk to others or disappear for more drinks. In fact, as soon as she went quiet, he would ask her another question seemingly to keep the conversation going. They had the Grange in the morning so neither wanted to be too late home, so when Dee said she was going at ten-thirty he took his leave as well.

'Dee, if it's not too much to ask, would you come for a bit of lunch at mine after the group tomorrow and share your thoughts with me on ideas for the kitchen? It's not something us men are naturally good at deciding on, I understand if you can't I know it's late notice.'

'I'd like that Tom, thank you.' Dee felt shocked with herself for agreeing to go. She couldn't even blame alcohol.

Driving home she couldn't help but smile, she didn't want to, as somehow that might doom things. Could Tom be potentially interested in her at all? Or would she arrive and find his partner Joel sitting there as well; eager to know whether to go for granite worktops or oak. She had misread things before, jumped in and got hurt. Lots of times she had shown too much eagerness and it had scared men away. Rejection and abandonment had then taken her straight back to her unhappy playground days. Dee put the radio on and turned to a classical music station; she needed to clear her mind and calm herself. By the time she got home she had determined that Tom was not interested in her sexually but saw her as one of his gang of like-minded country bumpkins, interested in saving heritage in the form of stone walls and cottage kitchens. After all, why would he be interested in her? She was sure he had admirers, he was amiable and not at all bad looking come to think of it. He had a happy disposition and a confident personality, but despite that he wasn't full of himself. She recalled his eyes, pale blue like hers, his ruddy complexion was quite healthy and unlike many contemporary men he was clean shaven; none of those prickly retro beards. Like her he wore a jumper and jeans. Like her he seemed a family man, but he hadn't mentioned relationships past or present. She needed to find out, as a matter of urgency, what his present status was. As she pulled up on the drive, she said out loud, 'Actually I don't need to know at all, he won't be interested in me.'

Dee's mum had gone to bed, but her dad greeted her. It seemed his wife had taken too much fizz, had been sick and was now tucked up feeling sorry for herself. Dee's dad had put her a hot water bottle in at Dee's mum's insistence, but Dee declined hot chocolate. She had to dash to bed, she needed to sort out what she was going to wear for lunch the next day; such a dilemma when a girl only has a limited supply of jumpers.

Chapter 7

Saturday night at Melissa's was the same as any other night except that there was 'Strictly' which she had been able to watch and then 'Casualty', which was the highlight of her week. Geoff had indulged in too many beers and by nine had gone up, the only night he could have helped her with the kids waking up. It was almost as if he was living in a bubble, a separate life away from the children and Melissa. He paid them all only lip service now and he was a shadow of the doting husband and father he had started off being. It was just an existence for all of them and Melissa knew the kids' behaviour was worse because of the lack of attention from Geoff. The eldest was clingy with her all the time, complained of nightmares and was wetting the bed more. The youngest squirmed when Geoff picked her up and would wriggle and grizzle until she could escape back to Melissa.

She caught a reflection of her face in the hallway mirror on the way up to bed, tired and gaunt looking with dark shadows under her eyes. She had lost a stone in weight in a month as well. She lifted her hairline and studied her forehead to see if the bruise was healing. She flinched, remembering the shock of feeling Geoff's backhand for something trivial. She now knew she could not continue waiting for Geoff to change.. The usual negative rumination made her stop and say out loud, 'How can I start off on my own though with no income, two children and no support from my parents?' She gazed up the stairs into the darkness and knew she would have little sleep that night.

Meanwhile, Claire was still up in the early hours trying to piece together her past and think of ways to improve her life and the way she felt about herself. It was simpler for Dee; she just needed a man and a new job but Claire needed the love of the mother she knew she could never have. The bottle of red wine had not done the trick tonight, she still could not sleep. She turned on the computer and scanned the forum for self-harmers that she had joined. Sadistic as it might sound, she took comfort in knowing there were people out there in far worse situations than her own. Since joining the forum on Tuesday after the group, she had befriended an eighteen-year-old girl called Karis who had been physically and emotionally abused by her dad. From an early age Karis had pulled her hair out and then progressed to cutting. She had now left home to live with her boyfriend, but it was proving to be a disaster. Trying to rescue Karis had become a full-time distraction for Claire and as a result she had not self-harmed that week.

Chapter 8

Sunday morning should have been an exciting time for Dee, but she just felt numb. She was already talking herself out of the idea that Tom was attracted to her or vice versa. What would be the point anyway as it would only go wrong? She was so unenthusiastic she just put on a baggy peach jumper and leggings. Driving to the Grange she even thought about cancelling the lunch and making out that there were some crises at work and she had to go in.

It was a misty morning, but the sun was beginning to rise and she gazed at the countryside as she drove out of town. How she would love to be able to walk more, to see hidden woodlands and fall upon mystical clearings. It seemed an unachievable dream unless she won the lotto. Houses in the country were well above her reach even on a nurse's salary. It seemed impossible for a professional woman to still be able to financially make it on her own. Claire only managed because she had an inheritance from her gran who had left all of her estate to her.

Kate didn't make it to the Grange, after the party. Dee felt awkward among the older couples although Tom kept coming over and having a relaxed banter with her. He had already put the chicken on a slow heat and let it be known he had got up extra early to prep the veg. Dee couldn't bring herself to decline the invite and observing him talking to the other volunteers she thought how patient he was.

She followed his car to the cottage. It was only a few minutes' drive from the Grange. Pulling up in the driveway she had the kind of moment that Elizabeth had in Pride and Prejudice when she first saw Pemberley. The white stone cottage was postcard picturesque with an archway and thatched roof. Chintzy curtains tied back, adorned the small leaded windows and as she walked up the path a podgy black cat came running to greet her.

Dee walked through the oak door as if entering a secret world. Her eyes widened taking it all in. A red tiled hallway with whitewashed stone walls and a huge coat stand.

'If you want to freshen up, the bathroom's straight at the top of the stairs,' Tom pointed. 'Come on Mog, do you want to get by the fire?'

Dee started up the stairs enjoying the warmth rising from the log burner Tom had lit before work. She studied the family photos, a small round boy dressed as a pageboy and another in rugby gear. There was one of him with his parents, his mum with a short skirt on and high ponytail and his dad a full beard and wearing skinny jeans.

Upstairs, she should not have done but couldn't resist peering into the bedrooms on her way back down after changing. All the bedrooms were dated. They had flowery wallpaper apart from the one that she assumed was Tom's room, which was probably a Farrow and Ball heritage green colour with cream bedding. It overlooked the long garden which she observed was full of greenery, with a windy crazy paved path up the middle. There were fields beyond. All the doors were heavy wooden ones with latches. The sun streamed through the bedroom window onto the landing. Dee felt that the place had a good feel. She rubbed her hand on the walls on the way down, to feel the rough texture of the stone and admire its lack of uniformity. She took in the nooks and crannies wherever she gazed.

'Ready in ten, I've made you a coffee and now it's my turn to spruce up.' Tom shot off upstairs leaving her to watch the veg simmering, but it was also her chance to have a nose downstairs. The kitchen was a galley-shape, but she noticed there was room to extend. It was dated, with dark oak units and a tired looking Lino floor, but she then reminded herself that Lino was coming back in. Next to the kitchen was a dining room which you could knock through into the kitchen. The ceiling was quite low, but the exposed brick wall gave it charm. She then peered into the lounge which was on the other side of the double fronted house overlooking the garden. It had double French doors opening onto the patio and a huge log burner, next to which Mog lay asleep on the shaggy red rug.

She scuttled back to the kitchen just in time as the spuds would have burned. Tom raced in and turned everything off and asked her to lay the table while he plated up. He had changed into a pale grey sweater and black jeans.

From the beginning, the conversation flowed, all about their respective jobs and about Tom's plans for the cottage and then inevitably...

'So, tell me Dee have you ever being married or in a long-term relationship?' It was the question that always stressed Dee out. How much to hand over to a stranger, what would they do with the knowledge? How would she be judged? A no hoper, needy, boring and yes of course a loser.

'Well, I have had severa relationships but I guess there've been different reasons why they haven't turned out. Sometimes I wasn't the one for them and they started seeing other people in the meantime, or they've made it clear they don't want kids and the last one had a child but couldn't find time for a relationship. I have had a drinker, a gambler and one that was very controlling as well.'

'I am sorry you have had those experiences. It's hard to think how they could have treated you so badly.'

'What about you Tom?'

'I had been with Sarah since I was twenty-two, but after twenty years together she decided she needed to find herself and asked if we could have a break. She moved back up North. The plan was we would still meet every month for a catch up and we would still talk in the week, but after the first two months it was obvious; she didn't seem to be bothered anymore. It turned out she had rekindled a relationship with her first boyfriend. They had met at a school reunion and well that was that. The worst of it was, it was earlier last year in the February, and then mum died in the April.' Dee reached out instinctively and touched his hand fleetingly and smiled. They looked into each other's eyes and connected without saying anymore.

After lunch Tom showed her the house and garden and they strolled around the village. He pointed out where people lived and offered to take her to the village pub sometime as it was past opening hours by three o'clock. Dee felt relaxed strolling with Tom and they bumped into his neighbour Bryan who asked Tom to pop round for a drink in the week as he wanted some advice about developing a wildlife garden. Tom had introduced her to him as a friend. Dee thought how endearing the place was. It was the kind of place where potentially someone could slot in and feel a part of something.

It got to five and Dee was on an early shift the next day, so she took her leave. Not without planning a further meeting the following Friday night. This time Tom asked her to go to the pub for a pie and chips night.

Tom stood on the driveway waving her off and Dee felt sad to leave him and Mog and the small but perfectly imperfect house. She was reassured that there was a spark. She sat and watched TV recorded from the night before. Her mum had made fresh cream scones which went down a treat with a cup of tea. She reminded herself though that it was not good to have two desserts in a day as she had had apple pie at Tom's and she decided to try harder not to in the future. She grabbed a packet of Rennies and chewed on one. She gazed over at her parents and thought how nice it would be for Tom to be able to share them with her. Her mum looked back at her daughter and funnily enough she was thinking the same thing

That night Dee sat in bed and gave some thought to her self-esteem homework. She had completed the questionnaire about her present level of self- esteem and had started to contemplate how she wanted to change. She decided she was a people pleaser, always wanting to do things to keep others happy so that they would like her. This was often to her detriment, like when she agreed to swap shifts and ended up with too many late shifts at a weekend; or working Christmas because people had kids and wanted to be at home with them. She decided she wanted to feel able to say no if it suited her, without worrying what people thought of her. She also wanted to be able to rely on her own opinion of herself rather than relying on others to either compliment her or guide her. She also considered herself to be a bit of a perfectionist so that people at work approved of her and thought she was good at her job. It was exhausting though. She needed to be satisfied with less effort and achievement, otherwise she would burn out. Realistically, she knew it was impossible to be liked by everyone, but it was painful and vexing when she felt shunned or made fun of. It was hard to see how she could change and feel different. She knew she would have to though if she were going to make a go of being a ward manager.

Chapter 9

Melissa was having a good Sunday. She had taken the kids to Sunday school which allowed her to sit through a service in peace and afterwards Mark, the vicar, asked if he could have a word with her.

'Melissa, I have been offered a new posting in Northumberland. It starts from the first of April and I want to offer you the job of housekeeper. Will you consider it?'

'Oh, I don't know what to say.'

'I know it's short notice but it would give you and the kids a fresh start.'

'Geoff wouldn't let me take the kids miles away, or anywhere for that matter.'

'Well, give it some thought, either way you need to make changes, don't you? You have dismissed the idea of Relate or United Against Violence and Abuse so what's your plan?'

That night Melissa sat thinking, 'Yeah what is my plan? I haven't got one. Should I just go? Not tell Geoff and do a midnight flit? Is it the right thing to do?'

Until the early hours Melissa lay in bed contemplating what her next step should be and trying to decide morally what was the right thing by the kids, by Geoff and, dare she even consider, herself. It would mean leaving her parents and leaving Dee. Geoff may even be better off without her and the stress of young children. Hopefully in the summer, she would let him have contact with them all again. The idea of starting a job in a new town, with people she didn't know, scared her but at the same time excited her. Mark was a gentle soul of a similar age to her. She doubted whether he had any hidden feelings towards her, but she couldn't help, considering that potentially an attachment could grow. Then she would be the pillar of society, the vicar's wife. She closed her eyes, her head throbbing with ifs and buts and maybe's. Perhaps it was time to run it past Dee?

Geoff was also tense and awake, lying facing the wall. As usual he was worrying about what may have happened to any of his clients over the weekend. He had lost the young mum and her baby last year on a Saturday night. The intrusive memory came into his mind of his manager breaking the news. 'I am sorry Geoff; I am sure you did everything you could but obviously there will be a full investigation.' He wasn't the same man and he'd lost his professional confidence. Melissa had tried reassuring him and he often asked his manager for reassurance that he was handling things correctly. He needed to continue in the job. It was good money and they relied on him. He had hoped things would return to normal in time, but he had begun to turn on Mel. He felt guilty afterwards, but it was time to accept he was depressed and needed to see the GP and probably someone to talk to.

Geoff, however, had been brought up not to show weakness. As he lay there, he decided that he wouldn't tell Melissa any more about this as it would only worry her. He would just fix himself and get back to his usual self.

Chapter 10

Claire lay awake trying to decide whether to stop going to the self -esteem group. It would be for the best as it only hurt her brain. She normally avoided thinking too deeply, whenever possible. She disliked getting in touch with her feelings and would try to block them out. Sometimes she would zone out and then look up at the clock in disbelief at how long she had been sitting there.

She recollected that as a child she had spent long periods just sitting on her own in the bedroom, watching the rain against the window or looking at patterns in the curtains and thinking they were faces. Her mum would always be out here and there and spent little quality time with Claire. When she moved to live with her gran, the same happened and gran would always have a lengthy kip after lunch while Claire would sit staring at the fire flickering in the hearth. She would fantasise, a lot, that she had a different life, she would pretend to be a beautiful and popular pop star and would dance around her bedroom holding a hairbrush and singing into it.

As a teenager Claire had friends but things were often complicated. They were often bitchy to her, because of how attractive she was, and they distanced themselves when they got boyfriends for fear that she would steal their boy.

She had lost a couple of close friends when the incident with her mum's boyfriend happened. They didn't believe her and thought she was attention seeking. She still had two of her oldest friends, but she felt they distanced themselves a bit and she never had the money to go out shopping or later clubbing. Claire threw herself more into her GCSE's and then A Levels as she felt this and restricting her diet by purging was the only thing in life she could control.

Then Claire found cutting and that became her biggest coping strategy as a way of releasing emotions and punishing herself for being who she was - the person people did not want to be with, the drama queen. She herself, had wanted to believe that she had somehow misinterpreted John's actions. She had tried so hard after that night to feel normal and to feel that her mum still accepted her. Sadly, no amount of A grade exams and admiration from boys made her happy or impressed her mum. Desperately lonely she moved away to university to do a nursing course. She had narrowly missed out on the right grades to do medicine.

Chapter 11

It was always difficult for health care professionals after a weekend., returning to work and wondering who had passed over. It made Dee think about the fragility of life. The months and years were going quickly. She needed to have a child soon. She often thought about the agony of being a mother, the physical stress of childbirth, the emotional stress of dealing with teenage toxicity and the ultimate betrayal of the offspring fleeing the nest. She saw it on the TV and read about it on problem pages. It was a journey fraught with potholes. Was it worth the risk?

'Nurse, I am sorry to bother you, I know you're busy, but I need the commode.'

'Nurse, can you tell me if the doctor will see my dad today?'

'Nurse, am I going to die?'

As usual, she left the hospital about half an hour late. It took ages to type up what had happened to the patient's that day and what needed to be done; a necessity though in case they died as soon as you left the ward and people needed someone to blame.

Dee's dad always cooked on a Monday. That day it was

stew and dumplings which was her favourite. She looked at her parents' faces, both nearly sixty and a little tired looking but both healthy. Surprising she thought after the countless years of chauffeuring her around often late at night after Saturday jobs in bars, or to and from her dancing and singing lessons. They had spent endless long nights supplying her with cups of tea when she was revising and counselling her that she was pretty, and others were just jealous. What was she giving them in return? Seventy pounds a week board. They should have a grandchild by now.

'Mum and Dad, I just want to say that I do appreciate all you have done for me over the years and all you still do. I love you both very much.'

Dee's mum's eyes welled up and her dad coughed a little.

'You're welcome, you have always been worth it,' her mum squeezed Dee's hand over the dinner table.

'Shall I get the Monopoly board out?' her dad enthused. As always, in his mind, Dee was still about ten.

Later that night Dee received a text from Melissa to arrange a girlie catchup Thursday morning with no kids this time. 'Great,' Dee thought, 'I can fill her in on Tom.' Talking of whom it was eight, and he would be expecting her to Facetime.

'Hi, how are you doing today?' Tom said, standing next to a bookshelf by the door. 'I've rescued it from the Grange, a good varnish and I thought it would go nicely in the nook at the top of the stairs. It will make a little quiet area to read. What do you think?'

'Tom it's beautiful. It will look great without the varnish; more rustic looking.'

'Even better if we can get away without doing it,' he looked down for a moment realizing that he had said; 'we.'

'What books do you like reading Tom?'

'Crime but I want to try some of the classics. They're on my bucket list so I need to crack on.'

'You're a bit young for a bucket list.'

'Well after losing dad at an early age and then mum's accident last year, it makes you think more about your own future.'

'I'm sorry Tom, I should have thought before I said that. I didn't mean to be insensitive.'

'No, it wasn't. Anyway, what's on your bucket list or haven't you got one?'

'I want to have a child as soon as possible.' She looked for a reaction in Tom. No women's magazine would ever advocate telling a potential partner of any desire for children or marriage but, hey, she was 35 and tired of wasting time.

'Great, I had been mentioning that to Sarah for at least five years before we split up; dropping hints but she never used to comment. My neighbours are foster carers, and I am always around there. They have twin boys now; they're sixteen months old.'

'Really, how does she cope though when she has to hand them back?'

'She's only doing long-term fostering now; this pair won't go back.'

'What are your neighbours called? They sound amazing people.'

'Julia and Patrick. They are in their late forties now, as well. Would you like to meet them when we go to the pub Friday night? They usually nip in.'

'Yeah, great.'

'Dee, I was thinking, and no pressure and please don't get me wrong; but how about you stay over Friday night? I will make up mum's old room for you to sleep in; it's just that I would love to show you the deer park at dawn.'

'I would love to see that.'

Sitting up in bed later that night she thought they must be in the 'talking' stage of things. This can be a prolonged period and can of course include sexual intimacy before you decide whether you are in a relationship. A relationship is when you change your profile picture and Facebook status so everyone knows. Was Tom for real? He owned a cottage, wanted a child and had free access to a deer park at dawn. She felt a 'Sleepless in Seattle' moment coming on. That must only mean one thing though - something was going to go wrong.

'Hi,' Dee said scrambling into Claire's car on Tuesday night to go to the group. She then went on to tell Claire how things had progressed with Tom.

'I'm pleased for you Dee; it sounds like he's 'normal' if you know what I mean. Just take it easy and see how it goes. You always wanted a chocolate box cottage. Does it have a rose around it?'

'Not yet. How's things with you? Any luck with the self-harm website?'

'I haven't done any this week; I'm trying to say a positive mantra to myself whenever I feel like self-harming and then distract myself.' She omitted to mention the red wine intake which had partly replaced the cutting.

Joy, the group-leader, was eager to receive their self-esteem questionnaires, so that she could compare them with their score at the end of the group to see if their self-esteem had improved. At least five members had not attended. Joy wasn't surprised. Attending a group when you have low self-esteem was a big ask.

'Right then, does anyone want to feedback anything about how they feel their self-esteem is now and how they want to change?'

The group were silent and many looked at the floor. Dee looked around and saw broken faces. The kind of expressions that said, 'What is the point in this, I am never going to change.' She overwhelmingly felt an urge to say something that might give others the confidence to speak.

'Well from an early age I never felt good enough, or likeable. It started off as a body image thing as I was chubby as a kid and now for that matter. I never felt I fitted in and that people wanted me around. I still struggle now with the same feelings. So, I would like to not worry about whether people like me, or whether people feel I am good enough,' Dee said tentatively, worried, as soon as she said it, how others would react.

A couple of others then fed back in agreement with Dee's views. Claire started to zone out and was looking at the picture on the wall. Joy must have noted this and gently encouraged her to speak.

'I want to feel I am not a bad person,' Claire blurted out and then had the impulse to run out of the room and cut but, as if sensing this, Joy stood and gently touched her shoulder encouraging her to stay.

'Alright, well tonight we are going to think about how we got low self-esteem issues. This can be emotional and no one has to talk about their own experiences, but we are going to look at things broadly.'

Dee and Claire met each other's eyes as if they were both being frog marched to stand in front of a firing squad.

'Okay, if any of you start to feel tearful or angry, take a moment outside and I will also offer additional support to you after the session. We don't have to do this in depth but nevertheless it's important we accept how we got to where we are now.'

'As a child it may have been that we were bullied emotionally or physically by friends, family, or teachers. We may have been picked on owing to the way we looked, because of our nationality, religion, culture, social standing or because of our academic prowess or lack of it or endless other things. We may not have felt heard or understood. We may have been belittled, called names, told we were rubbish, ugly, fat, laughed at, told to go away and that no one wanted to be your friend. People who we believed should be kind to us like teachers or parents or best friends, let us down.'

It was hard for Joy as she knew, by saying this, that attendees would immediately tap into memories of when this had happened to them. As she looked around the room, people were busily wiping their eyes or looking at the floor. She looked at Dee, whose eyes were streaming.

Dee was remembering being back in the playground. Her friend Hannah had said to her, 'My mum says you can come out to the cinema next time. There's not enough room in the car this time.'

Joy continued, 'Some of you may have had parents who split up and the sense of loss and lack of contact with the absent parent may have damaged your confidence, given you a feeling of rejection or abandonment. Children have a knack of blaming themselves when parents split up and too often things are hidden or unspoken. Sometimes having to get used to step-parents and step-siblings, leaves people feeling they had less importance to the parent thereafter. They had to share their parent with other kids.'

'Sibling rivalry with blood or step siblings is another big cause of low self-esteem, if you compare yourselves unfavourably with them. Perhaps they were more clever, sportier, more popular; more beautiful. Perhaps parents seemed to show more affection towards them and you were the one to get told off all the time or physically chastised. Some of you may have been brought up by parents who also had self-esteem issues, they did not socialize you or teach you to stand up for yourself.'

Around the room there were sniffles, people getting up to use the toilet and sounds of noses been blown. People were shuffling in their seats, looking at the floor and, as for Claire, her eyes were fixed on the swirly patterns on the curtains. She could see evil faces staring back.

'Some of you may have been left on your own to fend for yourselves or may have had to caretake parents who put their own needs before yours. Some of you may have been sexually abused by people you thought you could trust and you may have felt like you were not believed.'

Dee looked at Claire expecting her to head for the door at this point, but Claire had already left the room and gone into her other world.

'Things in later life also affect your self- esteem. Some of you may have been involved in abusive relationships, may have suffered crimes, or bullying at work, divorces and redundancies, all affect self- esteem.

'Let's not dwell though on what caused us to have low self- esteem but move on to understanding our own self-esteem issues. It's important to think about what our core beliefs about ourselves are, other people and the world around us. This can be difficult for us to do. One way to do this is to think of incidents when we have been upset, angry, frightened or have had any other strong negative emotion. This is usually when one of our core beliefs has been set off or "triggered", as we say in the business.'

'Example, you may be watching the news and find out that someone who has committed a sexual assault got a suspended sentence. You may react with "life's so unfair". It could be that you often have that belief and so that would be a core belief.

'Another example may be that your boss has praised a colleague in front of you and you may feel upset they haven't praised you. You may then believe "I am not as good as others, or I am unlikeable".

'I will give you a list of common core beliefs to help guide you, but it isn't exhaustive.'

The list included, I am unattractive, boring, unlikeable, unlovable, different to others, I am a bad person, I am guilty, selfish, unreliable, untrustworthy, unlucky, useless....

Other people are selfish, luckier than me, cleverer than me, more attractive, more popular, more interesting, have more get up and go, untrustworthy, others are out to get me, to use me, others let you down.

'The world is safe, unsafe, unfair, despicable.

'So why do we need to know what our core beliefs are? We need to learn to analyse them and challenge the evidence as to whether our core beliefs are true. If they are, well can we work around them better, so they are not so debilitating and distressing for us.

'Homework then is to make a list of our core beliefs, about ourselves, about others in general and the world in general.'

The two friends drove home together discussing what they thought their own beliefs were.

'Well, mine are easy Claire, I don't ever feel good enough and doubt that people really like me. I even wonder whether you and Melissa just tolerate me.'

'Blimey Dee, you shouldn't doubt what we think of you. How long have we been friends for now?'

'What about your beliefs then Claire?'

'I guess mine are more about other people not being trustworthy and out to get what they want. That's why I worry about having a relationship; eventually I think they will leave me just like mum did. The other thing is, I worry I am a bad person. I must be if my mum doesn't want anything to do with me and blames me for what happened between me and John.'

'I will always be here for you Claire and you are not a bad person.'

'Well, there's something I want to tell you about; I'm thinking about going to work for the Red Cross. They need nurses in the refugee camps in Syria. I am thinking of taking a year off work to go, you know reinvent myself. I might not even come back to work.'

Dee looked at her friend not knowing what to say. Dee desperately wanted to tell Claire not to go but being a good friend, said 'It may be worth thinking about.'

Chapter 12

Thursday morning and Dee arrived at the meeting place where she always met Melissa. They had not had a proper girlie catch up without the kids, for ages, so Dee was really looking forward to it.

The two friends had been going to the same café since they were teenagers. The old torn wallpaper and brown checked carpet had recently been replaced with a minimalist gardenia coloured whitewash, acorn-brown vinyl, tub chairs and there was a new owner called Ash. It was all new. They preferred the old place and the old prices. Instead of a bacon cob it was now a hummus wrap. The smell of the place had improved though. The mustiness had gone and there was the aroma of coffee.

'Dee, I have something to tell you. I've wanted to for some time, but I've felt frightened to. It's about Geoff. Well, I am not sure where to start, but he has changed, you see. He's started to drink.' Melissa struggled to hold eye contact with Dee and was waiting for a reaction before disclosing more.

'Oh, I'm sorry Mel. What is he doing about it? Why haven't you mentioned it before?' Dee studied the expression on Mel's face. Then she saw her part her hair and just on the hairline; the yellow bruise came into view. The two friends sat staring at one another.

'Oh my God Mel. No, not Geoff?' Dee reached over and grabbed Mel's hands and clasped them firmly in her own.

'How long as this been happening? He isn't having a go at the kids as well, is he?'

'No, he just avoids the kids and now they're suffering because of it. It has been happening since about three months after the thing at work. It's when he's had a few, he gets kind of leery and digs at me about the house looking a mess. He's always tired and moody. I try to stick up for myself and that's when he loses it. So now I am just trying to keep out his way. I let him say his piece and say sorry or say nothing. It's easier...'

'I can't believe you haven't said anything before. I could have spoken to him, is he hitting you in front of the kids?'

'Well, because you're a nurse, Dee, and with child protection and everything, that's why I never said anything. I didn't want social services coming round. I love my kids Dee. I can't lose my kids. He has never done it in front of them as they're normally in bed. He only drinks at night, you see.' Mel threw her head in her hands in anguish.

'Is he going for help to stop drinking?' Dee slipped into

problem solving mode - an inbuilt default button for all nurses.

'No, he doesn't think he's got a problem. I guess he blames me for winding him up or allowing the kids to.'

'Melissa, do you want me to talk to him about things and encourage him to get some help?'

'No Dee. I have decided I don't want him anymore. I don't want this life anymore. I am going away.'

'Going away where? What about the kids they still need to have contact with their dad?'

'The kids will be better off without him in their lives. He can visit sometimes in school holidays and he can Facetime and stuff, but I don't know if he'll be bothered to.' Melissa clenched her teeth in resignation at her situation.

'Mel where are you going? I can't take it all in. I can't imagine Geoff like this and I feel you're being a little hasty. Geoff has always been there for you until now. No marriage is perfect and sometimes you do have to bumble along together. What he is doing is wrong, but that investigation has obviously made him mentally unwell.'

'Dee, I know you mean well, but what about me and the kids and the effect it's having on us? How do I know the next time he won't hit me a little too hard and, well, I die?'

'Melissa speak to him, give him a chance to say he'll get counselling or threaten to leave; perhaps he'll be motivated then?'

'I've said that to him, God only knows how many times, he just tells me he doesn't need help. If only the house was calmer, if only the work was not so stressful. If only the investigation hadn't happened. It's everyone else's fault but his own.'

'But Mel, he'll be heartbroken and how will you manage on your own?'

'I won't be on my own.'

'I've got a job as a housekeeper for the vicar Mark. He has a new placement out of the area.'

'You have to be able to look the kids in the eye when they're eighteen and justify what you are doing. You're taking them away and you are giving up on their dad. Can't you just ask Geoff to leave and live separately for a while and see how things go. See if he can get help?'

Mel's jaw hardened, 'Don't you see he's the one who's giving up on us.'

They had known each other for nearly twenty-five years but now they looked across the table uncomfortably at one another. Dee could see that Melissa was hurt but Dee, believed that the meaning of marriage and family was about supporting one another through the tough times and not giving up. She was disgusted with Geoff, but he was obviously deeply troubled; probably mentally ill and his wife was abandoning him.

'Just keep thinking it over Mel. If you do go, well how far will it be and when?'

Melissa looked at the floor. 'I won't tell you when I am going, or where, until I get there. I don't want Geoff coming to you and being nasty with you, trying to find things out. Just tell him you knew nothing about it if he asks. You will be as shocked as he will be.'

'Why don't you prepare him for you going, so it isn't a shock for him. It seems a little much to do a midnight flit, if that's what you are talking about?'

'He will try to stop me. How do you think he will react? He will get violent with me. It will be a catastrophe.'

Dee felt her heart pumping in anxiety and Melissa's dilemma, 'How do you know he won't cry and beg you to stay. He might offer to get help?'

'Because I have tried it before. Threatening to leave doesn't work. He then threatens me with solicitors and puts me down, saying I am not fit enough to look after the kids on my own.'

Dee clutched at Mel's wrist. 'I love you and the kids. How about you just stay with me for a while, you can have the annex and please try and sort things out. You will not just be leaving Geoff but me as well and I don't want you to go.' She felt her eyes prick with unshed tears as she saw Mel's face fall.

'You will always be my best friend wherever I live. You have great parents, and you are on the brink of what looks like a good relationship and a new job. I need a chance of happiness too. Please do not think badly of me. I need you to understand how awful my life is and how frightening it is when he gets into a state.'

Dee answered, 'I do understand. He has no right to take things out on you. It's so unlike him though isn't it, I can't get over it.'

Mel looked exhausted. 'Do you want another coffee?'

The drive to work was difficult. Dee's head was spinning. Her rescuer mode kicked in. She wanted to drop a hint to Geoff that Mel was serious this time, to prompt him to get help and quickly. She wanted to save the day. She thought they were a unit. She thought Melissa had everything that there was to have.

Perhaps she could secretly meet with Geoff while making some excuse up about planning a surprise girlie weekend for Melissa. She could somehow drop in the conversation a terrible story about a patient who had lost everything through drinking. Maybe she could stop this all happening. Or maybe she would make it worse, and he would twig on and go home and hit Melissa so hard for saying something, that maybe he would kill her?

Perhaps her role was to support Geoff when he found out that Melissa had gone and then encourage him to get help to get Melissa back or even to support him to get over Melissa and get a new life if they did not reconcile? She did not dare allow herself to think that the new life could even be with her, as she had always had a thing for Geoff since first meeting him.

How jealous she was and in the early days she had even attempted to flirt behind Melissa's back. There was always something charming about Geoff. He wore cashmere jumpers which always did it for her; until recently when she saw on Facebook how cruel the cashmere trade is to rabbits. It reminded her to drop a hint to Geoff to move to synthetic woollies.

Dee bumped into Claire in the corridor at work and revealed the story to her. In her usual unempathic style, Claire blamed Geoff and said 'Go girl' about Melissa doing a midnight flit. Feeling she should not have bothered telling her, Dee made her excuses to get back to the ward, as they were short staffed.

Talking to her parents that night, Dee found an audience for her belief that marriages often needed working at. She went to bed feeling drained and irritable. She felt a heavy burden on her shoulders. She was so tired, she forgot to answer Tom's text regarding meeting the following day.

Tom sat thinking that Dee was a good fit for him. She liked his home and unlike his ex she was not afraid to eat heartily and seemed comfortable in her own skin. No faddy diets and no nagging him to exercise. Like him, Dee had been misused and hurt, maybe this could be promising...? Why then was she not answering his calls? This was just how his ex Sarah used to be.'

Chapter 13

Friday morning came and Dee woke up feeling miserable and exhausted. She could not face work and just wanted to crawl under the covers and cry. Her best friends were both potentially leaving her. Who would she have to talk to now? She had seen and ignored the messages from Tom. Feeling belligerent re the whole idea of whether to have another go at a relationship, she decided to wait till lunch before deciding whether to cancel the pub night. She felt mean, Tom was kind and caring and had a thatched cottage but how could she commit to him with everything else going on? She messaged Melissa and set another meet-up for the following week, letting it be known she could always babysit if she needed her so that she and Geoff could spend time together. Then it hit her, what she should do; it was obvious. She would track down Mark the vicar and speak to him. Ask him to withdraw the job offer, to give them time to sort it out. She staggered out of bed to get ready to go to church.

There were two churches in Melissa's suburb, and she googled the names of the vicars and found him at St James. Entering the church, she looked round in awe at the stained-glass images and the highly polished woodwork. She found Mark by the altar.

'Excuse me Mark, I am Dee and I'm a friend of Melissa's.'

'Hi Dee, yes she mentions you a lot. It's good to meet you.'

'Look Mark, I know you are doing a very Christian thing offering her a job and everything, but don't you think she ought to sort things out with Geoff rather than running away?'

'Dee, I have spent the last six months telling her to get help from Relate or United Against Violence and Abuse, but Geoff doesn't recognize he has problems, does he? It's not as if she hasn't been trying to support him and I worry he will just keep doing it now, perhaps it's a habit?'

'It's come as a shock to me, I only found out yesterday and am still trying to get over it and the fact she hasn't confided in me.'

'Yeah, I kept telling her to talk to you about it. I just think now she has given up on saving the marriage and she and the kids need a fresh start. I have grown fond of them so I will support them when we live together.' Mark smiled at Dee. It was the kind of smile which really conveyed, 'back off now it is all sorted'. You don't need to meddle'.

Dee thanked him for his time and decided to stay awhile to sit still and think. The last time she was in church was her cousin's wedding two years ago.

She looked around admiring the heavy stained-glass

windows. She saw an image of the Mother Mary lit up by the bright, saffron sunlight. She studied the expression on her face, calm and serene. Just then it felt a further ray of sunshine brightened the yellow further. Was it a sign? Could it be that God was saving her friend by divine intervention? Who rescues Geoff though? Was it supposed to be Dee?

At home, Dee conveyed the story to her Mum. It was gone lunch time when they had both tossed the subject around and decided that this time it was not Dee's responsibility to rescue anyone, but still this sat uncomfortable with her. She hated secrets and still felt let down by Melissa's plans to turn her back on her marriage and do a midnight flit. She knew that Geoff was doing wrong but still felt Mel ought to give him a chance to sort it; even if they separated while he was getting help. This was going to be hard for her to reconcile.

Dee checked her phone Tom had texted last night and again today to check she was okay for the meal out. Her heart sank. She did not feel up to going, with all of this on her mind but maybe it was good to tell Tom about it, to get a male perspective.

Dee texted back with some made-up story that she had mislaid her phone and she would be around by seven and yes; she would stay. There was no harm in it. She checked herself. Why was she sabotaging a chance of something good just because of Melissa's situation? She knew why, but dare not think it.

Driving to Tom's, she was petrified that someone

from work might be there. She would have to say she had made a miraculous recovery from her feigned migraine. She knocked on the heavy oak front door.

'Hi,' Tom opened it, cheeks ruddy, as if he had been rushing around.

'Hi.' Dee walked in and placed her overnight bag down on the floor.

Spinning around quickly was when she really noticed him. Dee took in how he really looked. Hair tousled surfer style, manly chest covered in a white shirt and tall; taller than she remembered. He liked her as well. She checked herself. Why she was having a fantasy about being with Geoff when here was a man standing in front of her, no baggage presently, a cottage with a cat. What was wrong with her?

The pub was filled with locals. It was a typical oldy worldy place, but with no mustiness. Everyone said hello to Tom., They sat at a window table and ordered two pies and chips.

'You found your phone okay then. Where was it?' Tom lent over and stared into Dee's eyes.

'Oh, it had fallen under my car seat. Hopeless with it, sorry I will have to give you the home phone number in case it happens again.'

'I thought you may be having second thoughts?'

'No of course not, I have had some bad news though,' she relayed the story of Melissa and Geoff. Tom listened earnestly in between munching on chips.

He said, 'I feel sorry for them both, it's a difficult one. I can't abide the idea of him taking things out on her and I can see why she would want to get away; but it would be good if she could stay local so he can see the kids. Maybe he could get the right help and stop drinking and behaving the way he is?

Dee took a sip of her drink, 'I just feel there is something I should try and do to make her see differently, but I guess it's not my place to, is it?'

Tom said, 'Maybe she will reflect on what you have said to her already Dee, I guess all you can do is be there for her when she needs you.'

Just then a rotund woman approached the table, with such exuberance that it made Dee chuckle.

'Hi, you must be Dee. I am Julia.'

Dee smiled as if she had found a long lost relative. This was the woman who was fostering. She was intrigued to meet this woman and she felt immediately envious of her.

'Hi Julia. It's good to meet you.'

'What do you think to the pub? It's okay for a local and decent grub, isn't it?'

'The food was great.' The two women made light conversation while Tom went to the bar for drinks for them all. Julia's husband, Patrick, and Tom stood deep in conversation at the bar while the two women got to know each other.

'So, Dee, you're a general nurse. What a great career. I used to want to do nursing until I found out I had a needle phobia when I had my teenage jabs. So, I went into teaching instead. Worse move I ever made. Still I am happy now doing what I do.'

'How did you know when it felt right to foster? It must have been a big decision?'

'When I found Patrick, I guess. When I found myself as well, that's when I wanted to share us with a child.'

The men returned to the table and the foursome chatted idly, while the flames flickered in the open hearth. Dee could freely breathe for once, she felt comfortable in herself. Not judged. She felt like she belonged.

Arriving back at the cottage, Mog greeted them in the hallway. He rubbed against a giggly Dee's legs. She stroked his head and Tom asked her if she wanted a hot drink.

'No thanks Tom, I feel ready for bed.'

Dee sidled up to Tom and nuzzled into his neck. He gave a little huff and held her tightly. She could relax in his arms because she felt a little tiddly. He must have guessed as he lowered his chin to her and whispered, 'Alright?'

'Come on Dee.' He led her up the stairs and helped her into the bed, the same way he would help his mother when she was drunk. He wrapped the duvet tight around her and ignored her attempts to grab him and pull him in.

'We'll get up at six' ish and I can drive us to the park to show you the deer but we will see how you are; maybe we will have to leave it for another day.'

He observed at this point that Dee was snoring. He looked at her. An all-familiar sight. There was something endearing about her though, something almost tragic. Tom wanted to be her hero and rescue Dee. Just as he had spent years trying to rescue his mum.

The next morning Dee woke up startled. She couldn't think where she was and then the headache hit. She felt a sense of shame. She had only had three glasses of house red; she was such a lightweight. Stumbling out of bed she found Tom downstairs cooking breakfast.

'Hi, how are you feeling?' He turned from the frying pan and looked at Dee. Her hair looked like she had been dragged through a hedge backwards and her mascara was streaked down her cheeks.

'Selfish, I am sorry Tom we were going to see the deer and it's gone nine. I am sorry.'

'It's fine don't worry, maybe next time. Did you enjoy last night?'

'Tom, I really did. The pub, Julia and Patrick.' She walked up to him and hugged him. They stood for a while in silence, apart from the sizzle of the frying pan.

They sat in the lounge with the blazing fire making trivial conversation. Dee felt so at home, it was if she had never lived anywhere else; it was a strange feeling. She was due on the late shift but the following day she was on an early. 'Yes,' she would come around again after that...

Dee drove to work that Saturday afternoon with Julia's words resonating in her ears. 'I knew the time was right when I found Patrick and when I found myself.' That was what she needed to do now, she had found Tom and now she needed to find herself.

She drove back home after work with the rain hurtling down on the windscreen. She had to stop for a few minutes as the wipers couldn't cope and the windscreen was steaming up. She peered ahead into the darkness. In a week's time she would be taking over as ward manager. She now doubted the move. Was it really what she wanted to do? No, she wanted to be sitting having coffee with Julia, with a bouncing baby on her lap and she wanted to be snug in the cottage by the fire at night with Tom and Mog.

Sunday morning was a traumatic shift. They were one nurse down, probably too many uppers the night before, a particularly awkward relative, a heart attack demanding the crash trolley and a junior doctor with a God complex. As the most senior nurse that day, Dee was run ragged. She left the shift feeling used and abused and pleasing no one. She was tired and ached all over. Arriving at the cottage, she was greeted with the smell of roast beef. A hot steaming bath awaited her. She had forgotten a change of clothes and Tom supplied her with a long jumper, a pair of oversized socks but unfortunately no pants that would fit.

She relayed to him the morning's events. He looked into her tired eyes.

'I don't know how you do it Dee, any of you and without the thanks and pay you deserve. I couldn't do it.' He reached over to offer her second helpings of roasties.

'I think I am fat enough as it is Tom. I need to lose some weight and get fitter.'

'You're not fat. You have a lovely figure. It's me who needs to lose weight, but Sunday lunch is nothing without roast potatoes cooked in goose fat. Are you sure you don't want seconds?'

'They are delicious. It would be rude of me not to.'

They put a film on and lay together snuggling on the settee and then it just happened. They intertwined and then there was a kiss and then a tender stroke, then more passion. They ran upstairs like two teenagers who only had half an hour before the adults returned. It was not rushed though. It was thoughtful and gentle, as if they had never felt another person's body before and were discovering for the first time. Searching each other's eyes as they were exploring. Both of their eyes asking 'Is this the real thing this time? Are you the one?'

Afterwards they lay just holding each other as if they

were going to die in an earthquake at any moment and wanted to go together.

'Dee, I don't want to scare you away, but I feel you belong here with me. I know it's early days, but I want you here with me.'

'I want to be here Tom,' she lifted her head and kissed him tenderly. She had never felt like this before. It was just so right. Then the dread reared up inside of her, something would surely go wrong.

She drove home that night with a tingly feeling. Could it be that at last she had found Mr. Right?

She decided to have a heart to heart with her mum on arrival home. She had kept her updated all along about how Tom had treated her, what the house was like and about Julia.

'He does seem lovely Dee, but just take it slow. You have been here before haven't you and then it fizzles out.'

'Yeah, how do you stop the fizzle, Mum?'

Dee's mum laughed, 'when you know you are right for one another; the fizzle won't happen.'

Dee went to bed thinking about Tom and what he had said about wanting her there with him. It felt too soon but at the same time she so wanted to be there with him. A sudden pang of shame came across her. How could she be thinking this today when only two days ago she was fantasising about being with Geoff? Why would she swap the chance of forever happiness to take on Geoff and all the baggage that would come with him?

Dee's next day off was the Wednesday so Tom and Dee had agreed to meet then. Monday night Dee needed to put some thoughts down for the self-esteem group the following day.

Dee's core beliefs.

'I am not likeable. I am not someone people like to be with. I do not belong.' She thought about her childhood days and how this had played out. She thought about friends she had thought she had, but who then never bothered with her. Next, she thought about Tom and Julia and Patrick. They had made her feel welcome but how long for? Once they knew the real her... 'I am never good enough' was another of Dee's beliefs and she always felt she had to work harder to make people think she was.

'I am a fraud,' she said emphatically out loud. 'I fool other people into thinking I know what I am doing at work when really I do not.' She sat looking in the mirror at herself, wishing she could be a different Dee. A slimmer and more confident one. A person whom others looked at and wanted to be like. She sighed and sadly crawled into bed pulling the duvet over her face.

Chapter 14

Claire had been giving thought to her core beliefs in preparation for the self-help group. She had written down, 'I am not good enough. I am not worth noticing. I am a bad person.'

She started to think about all the times people had let her down, used her; and denigrated her. She thought about her mother putting her down throughout her life. Her real dad who never bothered to gain access rights after he split up with her mum. She did not even know where he lived now. She thought she must be a bad person because she had told her mum that John had come onto her and ruined the family set up. She must be bad and rotten inside to do this to them all.

'I do not trust people.' She thought about the times people gave her compliments and she dismissed them because she didn't believe them and she wondered what the person's real intentions were. She trusted no one. Why would she? However, she reminded herself of Karis and how she was beginning to enjoy building a friendship with her.

Karis had taken to self-harming at the age of thirteen after finding cannabis pranged her out. She had started the cannabis as her friend Liv also took it. Karis's dad was mean to her all the time. He would chastise her when it was really her sister's fault that something was missing or that housework had not been done. He would grab her wrist and tell her that unless she behaved, he would ask social services to take her away. She would try to answer back but he would ground her, and even not allow her a meal that night. He would barricade the bedroom door and not let her out.

At birthdays and Christmas, she would look on as her elder sister got bigger and better presents and she would get a couple of toiletries and a selection box.

Her mother would not intervene and would turn a blind eye when her dad started on her. He would taunt her about how skinny she was, how her breasts were small and her teeth crooked. If she wore anything too revealing, he would call her a slapper.

Karis had met her boyfriend Teddy when they were sixteen. He seemed to be both her best friend and lover. They just got each other and when they were seventeen, they moved in together.

Teddy worked shifts and Karis was still searching for work. She spent most of the day alone in the flat doing housework and had too much time to dwell on the past, present, and future. Teddy was a factory worker, working long hours, he also went straight to the gym some days after his shift finished. Karis had started to become paranoid thinking her boyfriend was seeing someone behind her back, she started to become jealous and controlling and then hit him. He never hit her back, but he would be critical and tell her to sort herself out. The more he rejected her the worse her jealousy and self-harming became. She was locked in a vicious circle.

Claire could vividly relate to feeling trapped in a pattern of irrational thinking and destructive coping strategies and was trying to guide Karis towards what to do. They had started to talk most nights and had decided to meet up soon. Karis was considering getting away from the relationship and focusing on herself, to find herself and get a job and to regain friends. Just like Claire she had an unavailable mother and sought comfort from Claire's interest in her. Claire seemed to get something from this, the thought of having meaning to someone; someone who thought she was significant.

Tuesday night came around and Dee and Claire relayed the week's events to one another. Claire was happy to hear things had progressed well with Tom but scorned Dee for approaching the vicar and trying to get involved. She was firmly on Melissa's side. She told Dee about Karis. Dee felt pleased that it made Claire feel useful and needed.

'How are you feeling about being a manager from next Monday then, are you looking forward to it?' Claire asked.

'To be honest I have not given it too much thought with everything else going on, but it will be nice just to work in the week; more time to get to know Tom. No late shifts either. It will be hard to adjust though, and I do worry about the reception I will get from the staff.'

'You will be fine Dee. I am sure they will all think how hard you work, anyway you have a crossover period of a couple of weeks when you will be shown the ropes.'

'Hello everyone, how did you get on with the homework? Was it tricky?' Joy searched the room for someone to start off the feedback. The group had now dwindled down to four. Joy expected this of course. It was not easy to analyse yourself; it was painful and risky. At first you feel worse and then learn strategies to make you feel different. There was no quick fix, no daily tablet.

'Once you know what your beliefs are about yourself, others and the world; you can begin to understand the way you think, feel and behave and the patterns with these.'

'We're going to talk about rules for living today.'

'So, let us start with a common core belief that many of you will have...I am not good enough, clever enough as other people.'

'Your rule for living maybe I have got to appear good enough or have got to strive to be good enough. I have not got to be seen as not good enough.'

'Behaviours could be either avoiding situations when you may be deemed not good enough. Like avoiding promotions, being on the pub quiz team; giving a public speech. Or behaviours may be things like over-compensation/people pleasing behaviours. Going out of your way to feel good enough, not saying no to people, volunteering to do things, helping people out or throwing expensive parties or spending money on people. Of-course it is about identifying your own behaviours, personal to you.'

'Sometimes, people end up with perfectionist ideas re body image, or feeling they must have the latest clothes, a new car, big house etc. It may be some people crave to do more and more further education, get involved with more volunteering or crave promotion and high-flying careers to try to prove to others they are good enough. The sad thing is even though you may prove your worth to others, you still end up feeling a fraud, afraid someone will see the real you. Still never valuing your own self-worth. To you, it will never be enough.'

The room was silent as people were deep in thought. The accountant, the two senior nurses and Mrs. V who was a prominent local parish councillor.

'Does anyone have anything to say, do you all relate to this?'

Dee and Claire stared at the floor, deep in reflection. Both women were feeling they were a fraud. Dee identified that she was both an avoider and an over compensator in life. Claire recognized that she was purely an over compensator: restricting her diet to stay thin, having a new car, a very overly clean house, a prominent job title. Just still not good enough for her mum...

'Let us try another belief about not feeling popular, likeable, lovable, fitting in, flawed in some way making you unacceptable to others.'

'Rule for living could be. I must feel like I am accepted, loved, needed. I must not feel rejected. Behaviours could be avoiding friendships, lovers, teamwork, clubs so to avoid the feeling of rejection. Or it could be overcompensation again as we discussed in the earlier example, going above and beyond so people accept you and like you. There is however another coping strategy, which is what we call attack. This is when in order to make yourself feel popular, you will attack others and put them down to make yourself feel better about yourself. For an example saying to your love interest 'it's your fault the relationship isn't working, therefore I am rejecting you as you are no good.' Unconsciously you are getting in there first, fearing they will soon want to reject you. It could be in work relationships you humiliate or belittle a workmate in order to make yourself feel king pin, so as to say.'

Claire felt Dee give her a sideways glance. Yep, this was all about Claire. Cutting remarks, quick to criticize, deflecting any self-blame and an avoidance of criticism; all to prevent not feeling good enough herself. Any new potential love interests were kicked into touch before the six-month mark; never good enough. All to protect herself from rejection. Now more than ever Claire wanted to cut. Instead, she dug her nails deep into the palm of her opposite hand and began to sweat. Dee noticed and gently stroked her arm. Claire stopped and focused on looking for faces in the swirly wallpaper.

'Okay, let's try a core belief about others. What about other's cannot be trusted, others are out to get me, use me, or others will use me and then leave me. Rule for living may be, I must not let others get close to me. Similar to the other beliefs there will be avoidance of contact and meaningful relationships with others. There will be attack behaviours if you feel others are getting too close, you will push them away. This is a painful belief of course because deep down you want to be close and have meaningful relationships but are too afraid to do so.'

'For homework, I want you to consider what your rules for living you have developed for the core beliefs you have identified and what behaviours you do. These behaviours actually maintain your core beliefs, they do nothing to challenge them, and they are going to be challenged in the course of our work together.'

'Heavy, isn't it?' Dee broke the ice first as they trundled back to the car.

'I don't see how we can change the way we are. I am beginning to think it's a waste of time coming, Dee do you mind coming on your own?'
'Avoidancy!' Dee chuckled.

'Yeah, avoidancy; but I get by the way I am. It kind of works for me.'

'Well, I am sick of doing the over-compensation thing to keep others happy or to feel good enough. I am not going to do it with Tom, nor at my new job. Things have got to change,' Dee said positively.

'That's good Dee. I think I will do the refugee camp, and this will be a new way of seeing myself. I will not be in charge, so I won't be able to put other's down to make myself feel better. I know you think I do that. I won't be able to go to the gym and dress nicely so I cannot over-compensate. I will have to eat what I am given so I won't have control over how to restrict my diet to stay thin. There will be no prestige and I will have to learn to trust people. Maybe it will make me believe in myself and not feel I need mum's approval. I have not even let her know my plans. I need to feel good enough in myself, don't I? It will also give me time to reflect on what happened when I was younger and perhaps it will change the relationship with my mum. Perhaps I will stop thinking I am bad.' Claire poured out.

'I don't think you need to go to Syria to do those things, but you must do, what you think is right for you. I worry how safe you will be, and I will miss you. Will you come again to the group next week? You may as well carry on, it might help.'

'We'll see. I am off work the rest of this week and I'm meeting Karis on Friday for a drink. So next time I see you, you will be a ward manager. See you Monday then.'

Chapter 15

Geoff had had a positive Tuesday. He'd met with the work counselling service. for an assessment of his issues. Of course, he had not mentioned his drinking or hitting his wife as he feared being disciplined and suspended. He had just discussed his stress and feelings of dread when he woke in the morning as well as the nightmares. The nightmares always followed the same theme, being humiliated by unknown faces; belittled and running away from the scene. Deep down he worried that others felt he hadn't done enough to prevent the murder and suicide involved in his case. People were supportive on the surface and said all the right things. Perhaps it was just him doubting himself and punishing himself for perceived inadequacies.

As a child he was often humiliated by his alcoholic father, put down and ignored. His mother was weak physically and mentally. From an early age she had often been bed bound. Geoff became her carer, taking her food and drinks in bed. He would dread his father coming home at night from the pub. He would demand his wife to get off her bed and cook for him, sometimes dragging her out of bed and insisting that she was histrionic and a fraud. His mother would plead and Geoff would watch as she slunk into the kitchen. Geoff would lift and carry for her and between them they would rustle up stews and fry ups. They would eat and his father would sit snoring from the drink. He would long for bed as an escape.

He grew up feeling he wanted to help other disadvantaged children and excelled as a rescuer and advocate for children in need of protection. He always found it hard to switch off when he got home at night and, at first, Melissa was a diversion for him. In a way he was also rescuing her, doing right by her and providing her with the understanding and validation her own parents had failed to do. He even enjoyed his first child as, of course, he was eager to be the father he never had himself. When Tilly came though he just felt exhausted and home became a powder keg. Melissa often felt overwhelmed and he would come home and have to cook and caretake the kids. He felt he was back to his childhood; back to caring for a weak woman. If he could just sleep better and could just learn to switch off and get his confidence back. He had decided not to tell Melissa about his counselling, somehow, he sensed she wouldn't be bothered to know about it. She seemed more distant. He knew he had to crack on to save the marriage. It would be such a good surprise for Melissa to see him back to his old self. He tried to snuggle up to her in the bed, but she turned over and yawned. He missed her.

Chapter 16

Wednesday night came and Dee was relieved to drive off into the countryside to see Tom and Mog. It felt like escaping to a different reality. Away from the organised chaos of work, the smells of the town and the litter strewn across the roads. She drove past graffiti on walls with no apparent significance, just done by some bored teenager in between X box games. Someone's shop wall, an old derelict building, neon colours ill placed among the rest of the environment. She watched people trudging back from work, standing at bus stops. Kids pulling for attention on their parents' coats and women with tired and drawn bewildered looks. Had they zoned out like Claire did? Dreaming of a better life or maybe just deciding what to throw in the oven for tea.

Although nursing was hard emotionally and physically, she wouldn't want to sit at a computer all day. It would be great if the money was better though.

She thought of her own childhood. Her mum had only ever worked four hours a day and school time hours. Her mum had always been there, meal ready for when Dee returned from school. They would sit together talking about the day's events and eating, then it would be homework time. At primary school, her mum would sit and read and write with her; she bought her a French book and taught her vocabulary. She wanted to be a vet and so they looked at animal facts and she would learn them and recite them back to her mum. They even did voluntary work together in an animal sanctuary. Dee hoped if ever she had children, she would be lucky enough to work part time as well. If ever she did have a family? Time was running out...

'Hi, how are you?' Tom pulled Dee to him and kissed her tenderly. For a moment she just wanted to stay, frozen in time. Feeling wanted, feeling she belonged.

'I am good what news have you got?' she took her coat off and hung it on Jeeves, the name she had given to the coat stand, checking her make-up in the hall mirror at the same time.

'Nothing really to report, other than I have ordered the kitchen worktops to be fitted in a couple of weeks. I went for the granite like we discussed. Oh, yes Julia came around earlier. She is debating whether to also provide a foster placement to the older sibling of the twins. She just doesn't know whether she will be too exhausted. The older child is five you see, but the social workers would love to keep all the kids together.'

'What do you think she will do? She isn't getting any younger and with the twins still being toddlers. Is it a boy or a girl?'

'A girl, her name is Abbie.'

'It's so sad isn't it, that siblings often have to be separated when they have already lost their parents.'

'I told Julia, that I would be happy to help out with school runs and things as I go past the school every morning. To be honest I think I would enjoy having a child around.'

'Why don't you apply to foster her Tom?' Dee said it without even contemplating it. She just felt it was the natural thing to say, but immediately looked embarrassed afterwards.

'It's funny you should say that. When Sarah was not showing any interest in having a child, I often wondered if it was because she worried about how it would change her body image. I started to wonder whether I should mention fostering to her' his brow wrinkled in thought. 'I would only want to do long-term or adoption of course. One of you would have to be homebased I think but I could be wrong. I would still ideally want my own child though.' Tom said getting up to clear the table after the chilli he had cooked. Dee jumped up to help, deep in thought about the conversation they had just had.

'You're on a late shift tomorrow aren't you, how about we do the deer in the morning?' Tom said in between washing the pots.

'Great' she smiled. 'What is it really like living in a small village Tom? What happens when there are fall outs, because I bet everyone doesn't get on all the time?' Dee pondered.

'Well, our village doesn't seem to have those problems. No one is noisy or disrespectful to anyone else. Most of them have lived here for years but newcomers are still welcome, providing they are not up themselves. Someone like you for example will easily fit in. You have a respectable job and you are outgoing,' Tom answered casting Dee a sideways glance while putting the clean pots away.

'Is anyone competitive though, like over gardens, or cars or scones?'

'Definitely not. None of us have brand new cars. The women all wear wellies and anoraks. We do have a summer fete, but it is low key. We all contribute different food and drink. If you are asking me if there's a lady of the manor who acts as queen bee, then no.'

'Julia is well thought of as she fosters and because Patrick is a mechanic, so he is every-one's best friend especially in the winter. Most of the others work in agriculture apart from Mr. Banks.'

'Are there any loners or is everyone sociable?'

'No everyone tends to frequent the local and so on any given day you are guaranteed to meet someone you know. There are less than a hundred of us in the village anyway.'

'My parents want to meet you, would you come for Sunday lunch after the volunteering in the morning. I am coming this week. I think I am on spring cleaning duties.'

'I would love to meet your parents. What do you think they will think of me?'

'I think you will all like one another. My parents are easy going there's nothing to worry about.'

'Do you want to watch a film, or are you ready for bed? You must get tired after being on an early shift.'

'Well, I do feel ready for bed but am not sure I am ready to sleep,' Dee walked towards Tom flickering her eyelashes and they embraced again. He gently stroked her hair and said he would be up shortly. He needed to turn the fire off and put Mog to bed.

Alone in the bedroom, Dee started to fantasise about becoming a foster mum to Abbie, living next door but one to Julia and having morning coffee and hazy days in the garden.

Downstairs Tom stared at the dying embers of the fire. He wondered if Dee was going to stay in his life for good. He speculated as to whether she would be interested in fostering Abbie in the future and giving up nursing to be home-based. To have a child of their own as well as Abbie. He did not want to come across as being needy and pushy, but he disliked living alone. He missed his mother and female company. He wanted to work for something. At forty-three he was not getting any younger and he wanted to enjoy a child while he was still youngish. He sidled into bed alongside Dee who had desperately tried to stay awake, but she had been up for sixteen hours and after the glass of claret as well; she was snoring. Tom looked at her and did not care. He lay aside her and rested his head on her arm. She was warm and, what was the word he was searching for, she was real;

there was nothing fake about Dee.

The next morning, Dee and Tom headed off to the Grange in separate cars so Dee could then nip off home afterwards and they stood and watched the deer. There was no one else around. They had the gardens and woodlands to themselves. Their own private world. The deer were out foraging for fresh grass, the stag, with magnificent antlers looked majestic.

'How could anyone enjoy hunting?' Dee pondered. 'I find it hard to kill a fly and will chase it around trying to encourage it out of the window before succumbing to fly spray.'

They walked hand in hand and when it came to parting, Dee suddenly got a lump in her throat. She now had two late shifts and so they couldn't meet again until Sunday as she had promised mum girly shopping on Saturday. When it came to Tom's time to start work, she didn't want to leave, and Tom did not want her to go.

Driving home Dee reflected on how quickly they had become attached to one another. It was not as though she was sixteen anymore and in love for the first time, but it felt like it was the first time. What if it went wrong though? She would not only lose Tom but the offer of a lifestyle that she had longed for all her life. There was so much at stake. She had fallen asleep last night. It hardly showed a lot of commitment from her end; but Tom was understanding when she apologised.

'We're not kids anymore Dee, there's so much more to a relationship don't you think?'

Dee drove to Melissa's house after nipping back home first. She found Melissa in a buoyant mood.

Dee hesitated, at first, afraid to ask Melissa how things were going in case she got a negative response. She was expecting that Mark, the vicar, had grassed her up for visiting him, but it would seem she was wrong. Melissa answered, 'amicable in fact at the mo.'

'There you are, perhaps he is acknowledging he has issues and needs to work on them?'

'Maybe, but then how do I know it won't happen again next time? You know next time he gets stressed, or something goes wrong - because in his job it's likely to, isn't it?'

'If's, buts and maybes. Have you reconsidered leaving?'

'Nope. I am still going, I told you last week I am not in love with him anymore.'

'That feeling can come back Mel, it's not as if you have got anyone else, have you?' Dee searched Mel's face, but it was difficult to guess her feelings as she had lowered it.

'Mel, you've not fallen for the vicar, have you?'

Mel carried on looking awkwardly at the floor.

'A man like that wouldn't risk a relationship with a married woman who is just becoming his housekeeper.

Can you imagine how his congregation would gossip?'

Melissa stooped down to pick Tilly up who was craving attention. 'So, am I not good enough then to be a vicar's wife, is that how badly you view me?'

'You know that's not what I mean, it would just be the circumstances wouldn't it? Anyway, are you not getting a bit 'Mills and Boon' carried away? He wants you to be his housekeeper.'

Mel had distracted herself building bricks with Tilly, it was not what she wanted to hear.

'Yes, he just wants me to be the housekeeper, but you never know what could happen do you?'

'Melissa, please just give it longer; you may feel differently in a few months again. If not do something about it then.'

'Oh, please I have made my decision. I am going and that's that, now tell me your news.' Mel gave Dee a baby wipe as Tilly had pulled herself up on Dee's legs that were now stuck up with marmalade.

'Well, I start my new job next week and have hardly given it a thought because of everything else going on. Tom and I are getting on great and guess what? He wants children. His neighbour, Julia, is a foster carer for two twin boys, but they have a five-year-old sister that she is thinking of fostering but she doesn't know whether she is up to it. The social worker would like them to stay together, if possible, but Julia isn't certain she can cope with three kids under five. Wouldn't it be great Mel, if me and Tom could foster her, and then have our own baby in a year or so?'

'And you say I am too Mills and Boon. Do you know what the procedure is like for fostering? It's really stringent and you are not even a proper couple yet.'

'No, but maybe Tom could initially foster her on his own and then eventually I move in ...' Dee said soulfully.

'Maybe, I can talk to Geoff about whether he has any advice, but you have only known him a few weeks, haven't you? It all seems a bit impulsive and abrupt. How long have you been discussing this together?'

'We haven't actually. He just told me last night that this little girl needs fostering and it set me thinking, that's all.' The two women then laughed together. This was how they were at school; they could laugh at things others couldn't understand; they just got each other.

Melissa made drinks while Dee bounced Tilly on her knee and stroked her hair.

'You will make a good mum Dee,' Melissa reflected catching her friend's tenderness in hugging Tilly and how patient she was with her; especially as Tilly was in Dee's face and interrupted them all the time.

'Well, if I make as good as job of it as you Mel, I will consider I have done really well,' they shared eye contact and both started to well up. Just then Tilly gestured she needed a poo.

Before leaving to go home and get changed before her late shift, the two friends hugged. They felt at peace with one another again.

'What will I do without you?' Dee searched Mel's eyes for any glimmer of possible doubt that leaving was the right action to take.

'You won't go without seeing me, there's Facetime and I should think a vicarage will have enough rooms for you to stay.' Melissa clung to Dee tightly. Dee was not just a friend she was a sister to her. She was dreading leaving her but dare not say it in case Dee bullied her into staying. She had mentally already left the situation; she was just waiting for her body to catch up now.

Dee arrived home and told her parents about Abbie, and Tom's desire to have a baby. They sat listening in earnest but tried to persuade her not to get ahead of herself. They had seen and heard her get too excited about relationships before and then there had been heartbreak.

'My advice, love, is to just make sure you are right for each other first. There's no urgency about children yet is there?' Roy eventually offered his words of wisdom.

"Your dad's right Dee, we are glad it's going well though, and we cannot wait to meet him on Sunday. I'll bake some scones and do an apple pie. He's got a good appetite you said ...', Shirley clearly relished the chance to show off her baking prowess to a National Trust Warden.

Friday was Dee's last day on her ward for nine months

or so. On Monday she would be wearing a navy tunic. Navy to denote ward manager. She had wanted to be a ward manager since she qualified.

Over the years Dee had felt proud and happy for Claire's success, but she had deep down felt jealous. It had always come back to the same thing; Dee just didn't have the confidence to apply to be a manager. Was it the right move though this time? She did not want to have to deal with any more stress as she was still worrying about Melissa and Geoff and the trauma of it all and then Claire was considering Syria. Other than her parents and Tom she was going to feel terribly alone.

Chapter 17

One person who was not feeling alone that day was Claire. She had met up at lunchtime with Karis and they had hit it off together. It turned out Karis was nineteen in June. When Claire discussed going to work in Syria, Karis also liked the idea of it. Karis loved the idea even more of having a parental figure in Claire. She wanted to be like Claire. She wanted to be beautiful and outgoing and have a new car and her own home. She wanted men to chase after her and to have the power to push them away. The two had discussed how their strategies to stop self-harming were going. Karis was now living temporarily with her sister. Her boyfriend had asked her to leave as he thought she was 'mad in the head;' after she had again accused him of being unfaithful. He had wanted to go out clubbing with his friends to celebrate one of the lads' birthdays. She didn't want him to go and so they got into a big row and he told her it was over.

Karis couldn't understand why he could not reassure her and why he couldn't understand the way she felt. After all, why wouldn't he go off with someone else, she was fat and ugly and thick? He had become tired though of reassuring her and living like a prisoner.

Karis had little contact with her parents now, wanting desperately to avoid emotional abuse from her dad and to have her mum dismiss it as banter.

'It's just your dad's way, his dad used to say similar things to him.' The intrusive memories of 'Why are you wasting your time with GCSE's? You know you are not up to it. Just get yourself a job' or 'Take that makeup off, you can't make a silk purse from a pig's ear.' The flashbacks played over in her mind and were often triggered by songs on the radio or things on television. Karis had little self-worth. It was Claire who had counselled her and she knew she needed to learn how to have better self-esteem before going into another relationship. Karis thought Claire was wonderful and Claire liked that Karis thought that.

Chapter 18

Fridays were often a late finish for Geoff. He scrutinized the events of the week and whether he should double check clients were going to be safe over the weekend, whether he had written all their records up; and what support was in place for the weekend? He would always arrive home late that night but with a satisfaction that things were as airtight as they could be.

He had started to talk in counselling about the events of the previous year and his perceived failings at safeguarding the mother and baby. No one thought they were failings, but he still chastised himself that they were. In fact, the investigation highlighted exemplary care from Geoff and the young woman had just seemingly sabotaged it. It was probably an impulsive act on the night following an argument with her boyfriend. There was nothing anyone could have done more. She could have phoned her mother and spoken to her; she could have contacted emergency helplines or the Samaritans. No, she chose the ultimate betrayal of herself and of her child.

Each time the counsellor tried to help Geoff rationalize this and mitigate his feelings of failure, Geoff would find some loophole, some morsel of if or but. Geoff was set on punishing himself forever for happening to be the social worker of an impulsive girl on a Saturday night after she had downed a bottle of cider.

Chapter 19

Tom was deep in thought about his future. He was certain Dee was the one for him. Not only that, but she had shown some interest in the idea of fostering Abbie. He had only just had the thought himself, so it was a good sign that they were so like-minded. He needed a plan. Financially he had no mortgage because the house was his. He also had had a separate sum of money in inheritance which meant he actually could afford to have a family and his partner wouldn't have to work if they didn't want to. He decided to start to raise the subject with Dee on Sunday. He would tell her that he was thinking about decorating his mother's old bedroom and ask what colour she thought would look fitting, maybe to see if she suggested a girlie colour. He would strip the wallpaper off the next day. He made the impromptu decision to call on Julia.

'Hi Julia, I know it's late, but have you got time for a chat?'

'Yes of course, come on in,' Julia always had an open door. Everyone went to Julia's for a chat.

'How are the twins?'

'Exhausting, but the walking is coming on. Patrick has gone to Bryan's to advise him on his engine. Do you want a toddy? When will I get to see Dee next? How is it going?' Julia's voice trailed off as she headed for the kitchen.

'It's going really well, I think. She's a lovely person and we seem to be on the same page.'

'You look well suited. She seems as easy going as you and she is very friendly. Patrick and I really took to her.'

'Ah that's good. Julia, what's the news on Abbie? How is she and are they still looking for a long-term fostering placement for her?'

'Abbie is coming on Sunday for a visit to see the boys, I think social services are hoping I will fall in love with her and just ask them to leave her with us. You know, we will just bring her suitcase in. Realistically though, Patrick and I have talked about it, and we think we will be too stretched. I know it's sad.'

'What time on Sunday is she coming?'

'I think they are bringing her around four. I said I would do tea for her and the boys and make it special for her. I am making cakes and will put the bunting up in the kitchen, make it feel like a party. Especially since her temporary foster carer has had to give notice, marital crisis. Poor thing, she is now waiting to be allocated a new foster placement and I'm hoping it will still be local so she can maintain contact with her brothers. I know she's only five, but she has been missing them apparently, and crying a lot.'

'Julia, I don't know whether to say this or not because you probably think it sounds crazy but...'

'You're thinking of fostering Abbie, or should I say you and Dee. ...Come round on Sunday and meet her and I will do enough tea for all of us.' Julia said knowingly.

Tom said, 'Thanks, but what do you think my chances would be of fostering, either on my own or with Dee? I just like the idea of trying to keep their little family together and you've heard me say how much I want kids.'

'Let's see how you feel when you meet her first. You should focus on cementing the relationship with Dee though, don't you think?'

They sat by the open fire, drinking brandy and eating fruit cake. Julia had a soft smile on her face as she gazed into the hearth and listened to the crackles of the wood burning.

Chapter 20

Saturday morning and Dee wanted to spend some time doing her homework ready for the group on Tuesday. She wrote the following in her notebook with a robin on the front.

Core Belief

People do not like me enough to want to be with me. I do not belong. I am boring and not fun to be with.

Rule for Living

To not be left out, rejected and abandoned. To try to feel liked.

Behaviour

1 Avoid work night outs when I think I may be left out. Avoid new friendships as I have got attached to people quickly and then they decide they do not want to be a proper friend.

2 People pleasing, saying yes to people and not challenging them at work so they like me. Being nice to

people and caring, even though they do not always do the same back. Trying to make jokes to make people laugh, or over reading up gossip about celebrities so I have got something interesting to say; even though it doesn't interest me.

3 Reassurance seeking- asking people if they like me in round about ways. Trying to read people's faces or body language to check if they are being nice to me and ear wigging conversations at work to see if people are talking about me.

Dee thought about her new job and how she could stop doing these behaviours and see if people seemed to like her anyway. It was a fresh slate starting somewhere new, she did not really know the staff on there at all so they wouldn't know how she felt about herself. She could try to act confidently and self-assured. She thought about how easy it had been to talk to Julia. They had never met before and yet they seemed to get on. She hadn't made an extra effort to make her like her. Then there was Kate. Although she had only seen her a couple of times recently at the volunteering, she had snapchatted a couple of times asking how the group was going and how she was getting on with Tom. Perhaps she could make friends who liked her? Still, she knew she shouldn't get comfortable and attached as this had happened many times before and she had ended up being cast off in the end.

Core Belief

I am not as good as others.
Rule for living

I must not make mistakes or look stupid in front of others. I must be hardworking and be noticed for this.

Behaviours

1 Avoid mistakes by asking for advice or double - checking things. Over writing lists of things to do. Staying late to do them. Laugh at myself first if I make a mistake, so not so painful when others laugh at me.

2 Over-compensation/people pleasing- Volunteer to swap shifts with others, stay late or do extra tasks that others do not want to do. Volunteer to do courses to show willing. Do not dramatise things if others are angry or stressed, be supportive and make them hot drinks. Be kind always to patients and relatives.

3 Checking, reassurance seeking without directly asking what people think of me. Looking for positive feedback and then dismissing it, playing it down. 'That's ok, it was nothing.'

Dee thought about how more recently she had been given a sense of achievement and approval. Claire thought she was ready to be a ward manager. Yet, Claire was her friend so had she just given her the opportunity because of that? Others knew they were friends as well so is that what they would think? This made Dee doubt whether she had done the right thing, but she had already discussed the issue with Claire before. Claire had said then, in no uncertain terms, even though they were friends she wouldn't have trusted her with the job if she were a crap nurse. The staff knew what Claire was like, they would know that that was the case. Claire took no prisoners, everyone knew that. Dee laughed to herself, no matter how much reassurance Claire had given her she was still paranoid that Claire was just bluffing. She started to think she should give the job a miss and make up some excuse to explain why she couldn't do it.

She facetimed Tom. 'I am doubting whether I am good enough to be the ward manager and don't know whether to tell Claire I have had second thoughts.'

'Just give it a go first, maybe it'll be something you enjoy. Think of the positives. No late shifts or weekends. More time for us.'

'Yeah, that's a definite bonus. What are you doing today?'.The picture switched to the bedroom with the flowery wallpaper, that he was in the process of stripping.

'Thought I would make a start on upstairs now I've sorted the kitchen out. Just not sure what colour to do it? What do you think? Something pastel to keep it light and airy?'

'Well, what about primrose yellow or one of these whites with a hint of yellow? What colour is the carpet?'

'I'll change the carpet. If it has good wooden floorboards like the rest of the house; I may just get them stripped and waxed.'

'Sounds nice. If ever you need a hand, just ask.'

'Well I was going to ask you to help me choose the furniture and bedding when it's all done.'

'Great, I look forward to it.'

'You know tomorrow, we have been invited round Julia's for tea if that's alright with you? She suggested four but I told her we were at your parents for lunch so she just said come when you can. Abbie's visiting her brothers. We don't have to go, it's up to you. I don't want to offend your parents by leaving early.'

'No, they won't mind at all, we'll have time to see them before we have to leave again. It would be good to meet Abbie.'

'Well, they're trying to keep the contact going with her brothers. Will you stop for the night?'

'Yes, of course. I want to. You can give me a pep talk the next day and take a photo of me in my new uniform like I'm starting school.'

'Okay, great. Well, have a good shopping trip with your mum.'

'Thanks, enjoy your DIY.'

Dee and her mum arrived at the shopping centre and her mum urged her into the department store. It turned out that, as a treat for taking the manager's job, she had arranged for a personal shopper appointment. Dee hugged her mum when she was told the news.

Jay, the advisor, was a trendy male with a goatee beard and skinny jeans.

'Hi girls,' he said chirpily. Dee felt frightened to death.

'Right darling, let me measure you up and start with you. Look at that red hair -gorgeous darling. Oh, and your cheekbones are to die for,' he swirled Dee around and swiftly measured what seemed every crevice.

'Now, let me have a look at your mum. Oh, I see the cheekbones are from you, I am so jell,' he twizzled Dee's mum around a little more gently. To him late fifties was ancient, and he was afraid she would fall.

'Back in a mo. Casual day outfit on the way and a little outfit for night to try and tempt you both.'

'Mum, I should be treating you. In fact, I will do. Let me pay for this.' She reached over and hugged her.

'Look, I am fed up of saving for my retirement when I might not even get there. Now and again it's okay to take a bit out and me and your dad are so proud of you we both wanted you to have something special to celebrate.'

'Poor dad he misses out though.'

'Your dad gets happiness from knowing we are together and doing nice things, love. We'll take him some beer home and a packet of pork scratching's though.'

Half an hour later and two coffees, Jay appeared with floaty chiffon blouse and navy slacks for Dee and a pair of leggings and pale pink long jumper for her mum.

Dee tried on the outfit. The blouse and trousers were almost boho style but flattered her body image. She was just so used to squeezing into jeans. Jay had fetched a pair of pumps as well, which were navy and white. Shirley was pleased with her outfit too. The women both looked at each other adoringly, it was not the clothes that were making their day; it was spending time together.

“Right my lovelies, now how about a little something for night-time?’ Jay floated the most beautiful eye-catching cream cocktail dress in front of Dee. Her eyes widened in awe, but then reality struck.

‘Jay, it’s stunning but I will look too pale.’

‘Nonsense and with a bit of fake tan darling, and red lipstick. Trust me girl, think 1930’s harlot.’

Dee felt she had no choice but to at least try it on. She rarely showed her legs, but surprisingly they were more slender than she remembered. They needed a bit of a shave though. The dress highlighted her cleavage, pulled in her waist and showed off her womanly hips.

‘Right, look at me,’ Jay stood with a tray of make-up and started to paint Dee’s face. He gelled her hair and tossed the curls back. ‘Ok, look now. Just need tan on your legs and arms, don’t forget your neck darling.’

Shirley had been sitting in the waiting area ready to see the finished product when Dee opened the curtains. Dee’s mother’s face said it all. Dee turned to look in the mirror.

She didn’t recognize herself. She looked more than a little pretty, she looked positively gorgeous. For the first time ever, she felt good about the way she looked.

Jay looked on, pleased with his artistry.

'Dee, you look stunning, let me take a photo to show your dad and Tom tomorrow of course.'

Dee felt vain but couldn't stop looking at herself in the mirror, viewing different angles. The face was good, now she needed to work on losing weight; then the body would catch up. Jay scribbled down what make-up he had used, makes, colours and the name of the website which would show her how to do it and promptly sent them off to the beauty department to buy it all. Shirley had decided against her evening outfit as she never really went anywhere to wear such a dress. She was just wanting to spend money on her favourite subject Dee.

Dee spent three hundred pounds in the beauty department and by that time it was seven o clock and time to eat.

'Mum, thanks again for today I really enjoy spending time with you. I know I always tell you this, but you are my best friend.'

'Dee you are mine and me and your dad can't wait to meet Tom tomorrow. Now what are we eating?'

'I think I'll have a salad and a diet coke thanks Mum. Oh, I'll pay for this by the way.'

'You don't want to lose weight before you wear your cocktail dress you know.'

'I think I'll be able to get it altered if that's the case. You know I'll probably not lose though Mum; how many times have I tried. I need to stop comfort eating when I am stressed and unhappy. You need to stop being such a good baker as well.' She chuckled.

'Maybe me and your dad will do the diet with you, and I will stop baking for a while. We need to lose a bit as well, now we are getting older. Don't want to pop off before your wedding eh.'

'Mum, do you think I have made the right decision about being a manager? You know how I worry what people think of me and I worry if people think I am good enough.'

'Pretend you are confident Dee, just like you felt in front of that mirror just then; almost think you are an actress in a film. Put on a show. That's what I often do.'

'Mum, do you think we were all meant to be who we are though? I mean we can't all be managers and successful in life, can we?'

'Well, I think lots of people out there who you think are happy with themselves aren't. I mean look at Claire. I bet there're loads of celebrities and politicians and people who don't like themselves.'

'I don't know if I can change myself really. I think I will always worry what people think of me and I think I will always want people to like me.'

'Isn't it natural to want people to like you and respect you and that though? Isn't it about the extent you go to in order to feel that way? I don't want you burning yourself out doing this new job. If that's the case jack it in and go back to what you are doing now.'

'That's just it though Mum, I don't really know if I want to carry on nursing or instead have children and be a stay-at-home mum.'

'You'll be lucky to not have to do some kind of work won't you? Most women have to at least work part time these days; I've always had to.'

'There's fostering...'

'Yep, and the country needs people like you to do it love but think about what potential stress you may be taking on. A lot of the kids are going to need a lot of settling down, aren't they?'

'We've been invited to Julia's for tea tomorrow, Abbie is visiting the twins.'

'That's nice. Dee, I hope you have found the one. Tom seems right so far and everything, but you don't really know each other that well yet and here you are dreaming about fostering. I just don't want you getting hurt.'

'Hurt again, I know what you mean. I just feel like, well I'm thirty-five mum and I should be settled down now. It's so unfair.' Tears began to trickle down Dee's painted face. She desperately tried to stop them, but clumsily wiped at her eyes and before long looked like a zombie.

'It will happen I promise you. You can always foster on your own you know, I read about that in the paper and me and dad will always help you. Don't forget you've got the money in the bank now for a good house deposit or we can look at extending the family home if you like. We can properly help you then.' As always Dee's mum was eager to make things right and rescue her beautiful red haired, freckled face little girl.

'Mum, I can't keep relying on you and dad. You deserve time on your own now, you've got retirement to look forward to when you're sixty.'

'The happiest times in our lives were bringing you up and, well, don't you think we want grandchildren? Most of my friends have them now and.. .', She bit her lip.

Dee replied, 'I know I'm a failure, not giving you grandchildren.'

'Dee, that's not what I meant, you know that. I just meant that we would help you and want to help you if you do have kids. We would never think you're a failure, we are always proud of you being a nurse and everything else about the person you are.'

'This is supposed to be a fun trip out, I'm sorry Mum. Do you want an ice cream sundae or tiramisu?'

Two glasses of prosecco later and Dee's mum was getting giggly.

'Come on Mum, let's get back to dad. I'll call in at the co-op on the way back and get his beer and scratching's.'

Dee's dad was waiting to help his wife in through the door and he encouraged her up the stairs. Up they went hand in hand, like a father taking his child up to bed. Dee's mum was cracking jokes and pinching her husband's bum. Dee watched the scene from downstairs. She loved her parents. She wanted what they had. She wanted a loving marriage.

She hung the cream dress up and fell asleep watching the You Tube video on how to do smoky eyes. She had to be up early the next day for her volunteering and Kate was coming so she was looking forward to it.

It felt like the middle of the night when Dee's alarm clock went off at six. She still had smoky eyes and now they were puffy as she had slept in make-up. She glanced over at the cocktail dress. What a waste of money. She could have had two pairs of jeans, shoes and a couple of tops with that money. She rewrapped it in its plastic cover and pushed it to the back of her wardrobe. She staggered out of bed. The heat was on but still there was a chill in her room. Underneath the hot shower she felt trapped. 'What am I doing? Dreaming of a new career, a relationship, children. 'I am and always will be just Dee. Good old boring Dee.' She sobbed violently.

When Kate met her, she gushed over to Dee in the carpark and hugged her.

'I'm glad you and Tom are getting on and you're starting your new job tomorrow as well, that's great,' Kate said in a high- spirited tone of voice.

Dee looked down. 'I'm not sure about the job really, I think it's going to be stressful and managing people isn't easy, is it?'

'No, that's why I got out of London and Human Resources. I couldn't switch off at night. I never left on time or anything,' Kate acknowledged.

'Do you regret leaving that job? I know you still work in an office, but do you miss the prestige and everything?'

'No, I get to work at nine and leave at five and then forget about work; it's good. Besides, I've got something to tell you. I wasn't going to say anything to anyone yet because it's still early days, but I'm pregnant.'

Dee hugged Kate and felt that she didn't want to let go of her. Not because she was so happy, but because she wanted to relieve the pain of the news. How cruel was fate. It must all be a sign. Even a new friend could bag a relationship, a cottage and a baby in a year.

'That is wonderful Kate, how far gone are you?'

'Sixteen-weeks. Still can't get over it really. Never really wanted one before but now I guess I feel ready. I am thirty-two so it's about the right time, isn't it?'

'Will you still work afterwards, part time or

something?'

'I'm hoping to do some audio typing from home, just at night maybe, with the cost of childcare and everything else. It's just a mad rush now to renovate the cottage in time, there's so much to do.'

'You need to take it easier now Kate, the cottage will wait.'

'How about you and Tom come round next weekend for lunch? I'd like to show you our extension plans. We're going to extend the kitchen as it's too small. I want one of those kitchen diners. Is Tom still doing up his place?'

'Yeah, he's ordered the new kitchen worktops and started stripping the wallpaper in his mum's old bedroom ready for painting.'

'He works hard, doesn't he? I mean physically doing work here and then going home and doing bits. We're going to get people in because we're useless at doing stuff ourselves.'

Chapter 21

Dee wiped the steam from the sitting room window and peered out into the grounds. There was Tom, in his old woolly jumper, shifting huge fencing panels around still laughing with the other men. He was so wholesome she thought. Just like her dad.

On the way to Dee's parents' house, Dee told Tom about Kate expecting and their invitation to Sunday lunch the following week.

'That's great news, when is she due? Does she know what sex the baby is going to be?'

'She's due August. I don't think she's finding out about the sex. Would you want to do that?'

'No, I wouldn't want to know but some people do, don't they, to get prepared. How long have Kate and Ben been together do you think?'

'I don't know but she only moved in with him in the autumn last year. I think they met online, didn't they?'

'Was the baby planned?'

'I didn't ask, but anyway she seems happy about it. She is just going to do typing at home at night when Ben comes home, after baby comes. They are extending their kitchen as well to make it one of those kitchen diners. I suppose it's practical when you have kids.'

'Yeah, we could do that to our kitchen; you know knock through into the diner. It might need a steel support putting in though.'

Dee wanted to say that would be great but was so taken aback by the use of 'our kitchen', that she didn't want to seem pushy.

'Kitchen diners are fashionable now aren't they, I suppose they are the heart of a home. How did you get on doing the bedroom yesterday?'

'All stripped and prepped. Do you think you could help me choose a colour if we go to B and Q in the week? I might take a day off, or maybe more, to get it done in the next month.'

'Sure, if you want me to. You've done really well to get all that done in a day. My dad's like you he has always done all our DIY and refuses to pay for others to do what he can do himself. Mum doesn't paint, but she does do the gardening, they do it between them really. If you want me to ever help I can now I have got the weekends free.'

'Great, we can carry on doing the house up together.'

'Are you nervous about meeting my parents?'

'Yep, I want them to like me and wish I could have spruced myself up more; but I hope they understand.'

They drove up to Dee's house. It was well kept with a bright yellow door and a huge container of flowers on the doorstep.

Dee's mum greeted Tom. 'Hello Tom, come on in.'

Tom presented her with a pot of grape hyacinths. 'I have just had a quick change out of my work – gear but would have liked to have dressed up more. I hope you don't mind?'

'Not at all, we're not formal here are we Dee?' Shirley ushered Tom down the hallway.

Dee's dad stood hovering in the lounge and shook Tom's hand. 'Nice to meet you, have a sit down while the girls just dish up. What have you been doing today then?'

'Well Dee's been dusting off cobwebs in the hallway and I've been repairing fencing round the deer park.'

'I used to be a builder until my back started to play me up and I had to retire early. I just do bits and bobs now, you know.' Roy almost sounded apologetic.

'Yeah, Dee said you would be able to give me some tips as I'm renovating the cottage.'

'Here we are, everyone to the table.' Dee's mum sounded triumphant. She was a good cook and liked to show off her prowess. This time it was Nigella's recipe for roast rack of lamb. Dee just hoped it was not drenched in too much alcohol. She didn't want her mum in a state again.

'So, Tom, Dee has told us about the new work-tops and you are thinking of knocking the dining room through to the kitchen. Roy would be able to help you with any plans and any advice you need, feel free to ask him. Ay love?' Dee's dad nodded while dishing up a healthy portion for himself. 'Roy has done many extensions and alterations over the years at work and at home, he built the annex for Dee you know.'

Tom sat earnestly trying to take in the conversation and munch on the food at the same time. 'Shirley, this is delicious, thank you for having me for lunch. I will have to cook for you next time. I do a mean chicken but it's nothing like this I'm afraid.'

'Dee's an excellent cook and baker, she makes fantastic light sponges. She can ice as well. She has always had a creative flair. The art teacher always said that at school, didn't they Roy? Do you remember that time she won the competition when she painted the cat?' Dee's mum always enjoyed showing her daughter off.

'Mum, I'm sure Tom doesn't need to know about a competition I won when I was ten.'

'Tell us about the village you live in Tom,' Dee's dad interjected.

'Well, there's a mixture of old and new residents. There are a few that were born there at the local farm, and, over the generations, cottages have been passed down. Then there's Julia and Patrick. Well, Julia used to tutor Mr Banks' kids privately. She said if ever there was a house come up for rent or sale could he let her know. It so happened that his elderly aunt had to go in a care home and so he offered Julia and Patrick the house at a reduced price if Julia was willing to take on extra tuition and babysitting for the Banks' children.

'Ah yes, Dee mentioned Julia and Patrick and the twins' sister is visiting today isn't she, Abbie?' Dee's mum, although worried sick that Dee and Tom were suddenly thinking about a child when they had barely known each other; tried to say exuberantly.

'Yes, I am sorry, but we will have to shoot off about four thirty; I know it seems very rude but we have been invited to meet her and I'm looking forward to seeing her with the twins. Poor little thing, she is only five and, so far, she has been with two foster carers since being taken into care. God knows what goes on in her head?'

'Yes, let us hope she isn't too traumatized as she may take a while to settle down and everything,' Dee's mum just had to get it in. Dee looked across and shot her a scowl.

'More meat Tom?' Roy asked in his unofficial capacity as the save-every-occasion diplomat and the conversation moved on.

'Thanks for lunch both. I hope you will come to mine

next time?' Tom shook Roy's hand and brushed Shirley on the cheeks.

Dee's parents stood waving on the doorstep. As the car sped away, Dee's mum turned to her husband and thought but did not say. 'I may be waving her off for good soon.' Sadly, she walked back to the lounge, avoided the school photo of Dee on the mantlepiece and wiped away a trickle of tears.

Tom and Dee left it till a few minutes past five to call round to Julia's. On entering the lounge, they could hear excited laughter and the sound of the twins rattling toys. Then she appeared - a thin looking, freckled faced girl with a ponytail and a pink fluffy jumper and jeans came into sight. She was kneeling next to the twins and showing them a book.

Julia got Abbie's attention by kneeling beside her. 'Abbie this is Tom and Dee. They have come specially to meet you.'

Abbie just glanced up and then smiled. The twins were pulling at her and she turned to talk to them.

'Hi Abbie,' Tom crouched down beside her and Dee took a seat to observe. 'Are you reading the boys a book, that's sweet of you; they like it don't they?' Abbie pointed to the pictures, she could not read properly but was gesturing 'dog' and 'cat' and making the story up.

Julia ushered Dee into the dining room to help her lay the table for tea. She had excelled herself, with bunting and balloons and cupcakes, trying to make Abbie feel welcome.

'Abbie's being picked up at six -thirty, so I thought we'd better start tea now.'

Abbie sat next to Tom with one of her brothers on her other side. She was trying to help feed him. She talked little to the adults but more to her brothers. Dee tried to make conversation with Abbie, but it was Tom that Abbie had taken to. He was constantly tickling her and making silly faces to make her laugh. Dee observed him in awe. She couldn't believe how comfortable he looked, compared to her own clumsy interactions.

'Why don't you take Abbie in the lounge and I'll finish off in here,' Julia ushered Dee and Tom into the lounge.

'Do you like drawing Abbie?' Dee reached for the pens and paper.

'Yeah, but I like gluing and sticking things more. We did a flower at school and I'm going to send it to my mummy.'

'That is lovely Abbie, what colour was it?'

'Purple with a yellow middle and I painted a buzzy bee on it as well.'

'How about you draw one now and Julia can hang it in the twins' bedroom, try and put your name on it?'

Tom, and Dee sat on the floor watching Abbie draw and helping her. They made a cosy gathering as the fire roared and Patrick and Julia looked on smiling and knowingly looking at each other. Dead on six- thirty the doorbell went, and the foster carer arrived to take Abbie home.

'Can I come tomorrow?' Abbie tugged on Julia's cardigan.

'Not tomorrow, but very soon Abbie.'

Then she was gone. Patrick took the twins upstairs for baths and Julia poured them all a glass of wine.

Julia noted, 'Well I think she felt welcome and the twins loved to see her, she's really good with them,'.

Tom was deep in thought and took a moment to respond. 'Yeah, she was really caring of them. Do you think she ended up watching them a lot when her mum wasn't around or whatever?'

'Could be, what did you think to her Dee?

Dee, staring into the fire, could feel Julia trying to mindread. 'She seems very bright and not as I imagined. I thought she would be quiet or in our faces as often neglected kids are like that I believe,' Dee tried to say it sensitively.

'You're right Dee, I think she was noticeably quiet and sad when she first got taken into care but gradually, she's coming out of her shell. I'll have her round most Sundays for a bit if the other carer can accommodate it.'

'Thanks for inviting us Julia but we'd better go, Dee starts her new job tomorrow and, well, we need an early night.' Tom hugged Julia and Julia turned to Dee and gave her a tight hold and then smiled poignantly at her.

Back at the cottage Dee jumped in the bath and put her pyjamas on, no sex before a new job. She began to feel sick and her head felt like it was going to implode. Tom had brought a hot chocolate up and she slid into bed beside him. 'You've done a good job of the decorating Tom. You have worked really hard.' Dee leant over to speak to him.

Tom rolled on his side and looked closely into Dee's eyes. 'What do you think to Abbie?'

'I think she's great, what do you think?'

'The same as you. I've decided I am going to apply for fostering and I am going to see if I can have Abbie. What do you think?'

'I think what I have always thought about you Tom, that you are one of the kindest men I have ever met. I think it's wonderful what you are trying to do.'

'Dee, I am hoping to write on the application that I am in a settled relationship and well that we are thinking about moving in together. We could then do a joint application. I know it's only been a few weeks but...'

Before Tom could say anymore Dee was kissing him passionately.

'Does this mean you're happy about this Dee? Am I scaring you away? I don't mean to be pushy. I don't want to risk losing you.'

'You're not losing me; you're not scaring me away; I just need to kiss you to see if you're for real and if this is really happening. After all this time, have I really found someone who accepts me the way I am and wants a normal family life, like me?'

'Yes, but do you accept me the way I am and well the idea of taking on a child and living with a cat and '

'Tom, this is all I ever wanted. Well, my own child as well and possibly a pink rose trailing around the front door.'

'We can plant one. I'll ring about the fostering process tomorrow and I'll mention Abbie and I'll get Julia to help me.'

'But Tom, I'm nervous about this job I don't think I should have done it. Managing staff isn't me, I don't know what I was thinking of.'

'Shush, just give it a go for a month and if you don't like it tell them you want to go back to your old job or just leave. If we do get Abbie one of us will need to go part-time or preferably not work at all.'

Chapter 22

Dee counted less than five hours sleep when the alarm went off at six. She looked across the room to her navy-blue tunic and then rushed to the bathroom to be sick.

Tom had gone downstairs to make breakfast while Dee showered and dressed. She couldn't resist taking a selfie of herself and sending it privately to her mum. Her mum had already got up early to text her good luck, as that was the kind of thing her mother always did.

'You look the part, except you're not rotund enough. Aren't matrons supposed to look like Hattie Jacques?' Tom laughed handing over a cooked breakfast.

'Ha ha, I will be bigger soon with the stress of it all, I'm sure.' Dee grabbed Tom around the waist and snuggled into him.

'When will you come over next Dee?'

'Well why don't we rendezvous at B and Q on Wednesday to look at the paint and stuff and then have a meal out? Then I could come back with you.'

'But that's two days away,' Tom protested.

'I will be shattered today and tomorrow I have my group remember?' Dee laughed.

Tom looked down. 'I get used to you being here and then when you go again the place feels empty.'

'Just let me settle in my job and then if you still want me with you, I mean to move in, well, I want to as well.' They moved towards each other and held one another as if for eternity, but it was only a couple of minutes, as Dee didn't want to risk being late on her first day.

Arriving on the ward, she was greeted only by the ward clerk, Maureen. Everyone else was scuttling around preparing for ward round later that morning. Mandy, the ward manager, apparently, was running late due to car problems. Maureen showed Dee to the ward manager's office.

Dee observed a dishevelled pile of paperwork on the tired, scratched up desk. Mandy's stale cup of tea now breeding bacteria on top of the filing cabinet and a calendar still turned to January on the wall. Dee, eager to be seen to roll her sleeves up, ventured onto the ward and bumped into a health care support worker bustling along with a commode in her arms. 'Morning.' Dee offered chirpily.

'Hi, I am Judy. Best get rid of this. Nina's in the end bay.'

Yes of course Nina. Everyone knew Nina. Claire had moaned constantly about Nina's sickness levels and about her frustration that HR had their hands tied. Nina, although a competent nurse, was never at work long enough to demonstrate it.

'Hi Nina.' Dee started assisting Nina with a dressing.

'Dee, how you doing? We are one down again today, Sophie rang in sick. Do you think you can help us out with the doctor's round?'

'Yep okay, maybe Mandy and I will do it together?'

Mandy waved Dee into the office.

'Hi Dee, damn car wouldn't start again. What did Nina ask you to do? Be careful, you know, offering to do things on the ward too much, even when they are short. There is a lot to do in the office as well. They think we sit about but there's always an audit that needs doing or a tick box thingy. Come on we'll have a cuppa and I'll tell you all about the place.'

'Shall we do the doctor's round later? I said I would.'

'Yeah ok, but don't offer again. We are always short staffed. You'd be out there all the time you know. They'll get it done even if it's late.' Mandy then started to give Dee the low down on the staffing on the ward.

'Right let's start with Nina. The usual issue is migraines they often start at fiveish on a late shift and then she will go home. This is regular. I suspect the after-school club stops at six and she has to collect her child. Difficult one, she is a single parent and has no relatives close-by. She relies on the good will of her friends a lot, especially at weekends and night shifts. She will often swap her rota to cover the childcare. Well, she has been told she can't have any more sickness in the next 2 months otherwise she will face discipline. She'll probably manage it and then it will all start over again, with new targets otherwise she'll be threatened again with discipline.'

'Then there's Sam. She is a skiver. She has a bad attitude and gets off on one from bullying Sophie the junior nurse. We all know it, but Sophie won't take it any further and no one will stand against Sam. She's such a cow.' 'Finally, there's Sophie. Let's put it this way. Well, it's like she has swallowed a manual on how to do things perfectly. The trouble is we haven't got time to do it perfectly have we? She is slow and pedantic. She has a good heart but never gets all the things done she should do on her shift. The others then moan, and Sam just digs at her. Then she goes off sick or locks herself in the loo. She often comes out with red eyes but when you ask her if she is okay, she says yes.'

'We've all been new nurses, full of textbook do's and don'ts. What support are you giving her?' Dee instantly felt the urge to rescue Sophie after remembering being there herself.

'I always try to ask her if she's alright when I see her and then of course in supervision. She is sick again today, Nina said that Sam had apparently given her a hard time yesterday.'

Dee had scribbled all she was hearing down in a little red notebook with matching mini pen. She placed it in her top pocket. The pocket that was to store secrets in. The rest of the day was spent looking at weekly audit reports that needed completing and by the time the day had finished at five, Dee was dead on her feet. Her brain felt it was going to implode. Mandy was right, ward managers had a lot to do and with seemingly extraordinarily little power or support to do them.

Driving home Dee thought back to when she had started her nurse training and how little paperwork there had been then. At that time, the ward managers were more visible on the ward, taking the lead with practical aspects of a patient's care. Surely that was where they should be? Out on the ward, stopping bullying, stopping complaints from patients, checking standards of care. That was what the public would want. A matron figure reassuring patients and relatives they were in good hands? How had it come to this, that they were just sitting in a poky office, doing rotas, filling in tick-boxes and being accused of skiving?

'How did it go love?' Dee's parents hijacked her when she arrived home; eager to hear all the news.

'Okay, I suppose, but there're a lot of problems with staffing and God only knows what the answer is. I am not sure, but I think I have made a mistake. It's not worth the hassle for an extra hundred pounds a month. It's not even prestigious anymore.'

'Just see how you go; dad has made your favourite pasta; I'll just dish up.'

Dee dived into the bath after tea and immersed herself in the steaming hot water until her skin turned pink. She felt sick. What had she done? She dried herself and stumbled into bed at seven. She was supposed to be Facetiming Tom, but she pulled the sheet over her face and simply wished she were dead.

At eight-thirty Tom attempted to Facetime her and she wanted desperately to ignore it but knew he would keep trying.

'Hi, how did it go?' Tom was sitting with Mog on his knee.

'Crap. Tom, I have made a huge mistake.'

'Tell me all about it, have you been crying?'

Dee went on to tell Tom about the staffing issues, all the paperwork and spreadsheets when she did not even know how to use excell.

'Dee, if you don't like it in a month just tell Claire you want out.'

'I'm not going to last a month Tom; I don't even want to go tomorrow.'

'I'm sorry love, it's not what you thought it would be.'

'Did you find out anything about the fostering process today?'

'Not had chance to yet, but I'll phone the agency tomorrow.'

'Okay, I'm going to go now as I am shattered. I'll call

tomorrow after the group,' Dee said in a resigned manner.

'Dee, I love you.'

Dee put the phone down. She had heard of course but she didn't respond. Maybe because she had heard it many times before and it had come to nothing, or maybe it was because she was so unhappy and angry with her lot that she simply couldn't be bothered to be nice to Tom.

Chapter 23

Tuesday at work was another crash course on record keeping and more tick-boxes. Dee was determined to catch Sophie on the late shift and support her.

'Sophie, have you got a minute?' Dee trotted after the young nurse and ushered her into the office.

Sophie looked alarmed. 'I've got a relative asking to speak to me, will it take 'long?'.

'Well, I just wanted to say that when Mandy leaves next week, feel free to come to me if you are wanting a chat. I remember what it was like to be newly qualified and having more experienced nurses sniping at me and how different the reality of nursing was from the textbook and that.'

'Thanks, I will. I'd better get to that relative now,' Sophie sidled out the chair and couldn't get out the office quickly enough. Dee looked at the floor. That was a disaster. She had thought Sophie might open-up, but it hadn't happened. Probably Sophie thought that there was no point talking to Dee as she was only a temporary manager.

Dee started to feel anxious, if the junior nurse wouldn't accept her then what chance would she have with everyone else? She just knew this would happen.

'Mandy, I tried to speak to Sophie to tell her to come to me if she ever wants a chat, but she couldn't wait to get away from me.'

Mandy lifted her head briefly from the staff appraisal audit she was doing. 'Nah, I catch her looking upset and ask if she wants a chat, but she'd rather talk to the health care support workers than me. Then they grass her up to me. There are no secrets. You know how big the grapevine is in this place. The worse of it is some of the health care support workers are in league with Sam and so she gets to hear everything Sophie has told them. Further ammunition for her to have a go at Sophie.'

Dee felt reassured that it was not just her that Sophie would not talk to. How, though, were things going to change if Sophie wasn't going to report the bullying?

It came into her mind, at this point, that her core belief about not been good enough or likeable was at play and that she was reassurance seeking from Mandy that Sophie had not rejected her. She tried to encourage herself not to seek reassurance next time and not to pander to Sophie, asking if she was okay and whether she wanted to talk? It shouldn't matter if the junior nurse liked her or not.

On the way to the group Dee and Claire discussed Dee's fears regarding her new job. Claire tried to reassure Dee. Nina apparently was heading for the sack if her attendance did not improve and Claire insisted that Dee keep her informed regarding her sickness or absenteeism, including going home early from a shift. Regarding the young nurse Sophie, she felt Dee could be good for her and gain her trust by offering to do tasks with her. Regarding Sam, she suggested monitoring her for signs of bullying behaviour and then they could go down the disciplinary route. Claire had it all sussed of course, water off a duck's back to Claire. Dee looked at her in wonder, why couldn't she have things sussed as well?

'Right then, feedback from homework? Were we able to identify our rules for living and our behaviour, avoidance, people pleasing, attack etc.?' Joy rallied by walking around the almost empty room.

'Yeah, I started a new job yesterday as a Hospital Ward Manager and I can already see what I'm doing,' Dee said in a resigned manner.

'Okay Dee how about putting it on the flipchart if you feel able to, with my help of course.'

'CORE BELIEF- I am not good enough and unlikeable.'

'RULE FOR LIVING- I must try to be likeable and be good enough.'

'INCIDENT- Tried to support junior nurse so I feel good enough as a new manager and to get her to like me, but she didn't seem to appreciate the offer. I was people pleasing and overcompensating.'

'BELIEFS- She doesn't think I'm good enough to help, she doesn't like me.'

'FEELINGS -Sad, rejected, worthless.'

'BEHAVIOR- Ask for reassurance from the existing ward manager as to whether the junior nurse accepts me, to check I may be good enough or likeable.'

'So how long does reassurance last for do we think?' Joy posed the question to the room.

'Not long,' Claire spoke up. 'I have been trying hard over the years not to reassure Dee, because it goes in one ear and out the other.'

'Right, and we tend to doubt the reassurance and say things like: 'they're just being nice to me, they don't mean it,' I want you all to start taking note of when you are seeking reassurance and how long it lasts and whether you accept it or pick holes in it. The message is that reassurance doesn't work, and we need to stop asking others for it,' Joy reiterated.

The group went on to look at other people's situations, when they had noticed how their core beliefs had been triggered by an incident and how they had thought and felt about the incident, and then how they had behaved. Claire had even spoken. 'My beliefs are often that other people are going to let me down or reject me.'

'RULE FOR LIVING- Avoid people getting too close so I can't get hurt.'

‘INCIDENT- My new friend Karis wanted to go abroad with me to do volunteering.’

‘THOUGHTS/BELIEFS- She is just saying this, she will change her mind. Why would I trust her? I am being used again.’

‘FEELINGS- Anger, sadness, bitterness.’

‘BEHAVIOUR- Avoidance of Karis for several days so I didn’t have to give her an answer on the volunteering question. This made her feel rejected by me which upset me and made me feel bad.’

‘Okay all, keep observing the times when you think you can’t achieve your rule for living. What incident took place when your rule for living didn't work or was proved wrong or contra-indicated?'

'Think about the thoughts and feelings that happen and how you react. Do you attack, avoid, over-compensate/people please or are passive and let it all happen without doing what is best for you? Do you seek reassurance, even though it is transient and short-lived?'

'What happens when you do these behaviours? Do you end up feeling worse? Do you worry what people think of you if you attack? Do you lose respect and care from others if you attack? Do you end up feeling guilty?'

‘If you avoid, does it make it even harder to tackle things when you’ve left it longer? Do you miss out on opportunities if you avoid?’

'If you are passive, do you end up feeling humiliated and downtrodden? Emotionally or physically hurt?Used and abused?'

'Is there another way of looking at the incident so you don't need to feel so upset or angry or whatever the feeling is you are experiencing? What are the facts about the situation that you may be dismissing? If a friend were in this situation and was feeling distressed, what would you point out to them to make them see things differently?'

'Then how could you choose to behave to get the best results? To get what you and the other person needs from the situation, a win-win for all. There are always going to be things happen in life when we can't achieve our rule for living and that's why they are often so unhelpful as they are too concrete.'

'Practice this for your homework. Stop and think. I know I am feeling upset, angry etc. Is this because my core belief has been triggered and my rule for living has not worked? Can I look at things differently? Are there any assumptions I am jumping to and ignoring facts? How could I behave to get the best outcome?'

'Now today's session is about the way that when we have low self - esteem we tend to predict things are going to go badly, that people are not going to like you, or that you are going to do something wrong, or others are going to wrong you as in Claire's example.'

'Negative predictions are what can maintain poor self-esteem. They are what makes us avoid things or escape things and therefore our self -confidence cannot be tested out. Negative predictions are what makes us aim to people please or over- compensate in order to feel accepted or liked. They can also lead to passivity, i.e. if my prediction is, I am going to be bullied at work then I may as well let it happen as I can't stop it as I am a weak person.'

'We can learn to challenge negative predictions, and this is how:

What factual evidence have I got that ....is going to happen?

'What factual evidence have I got that if it did happen it will it be as bad as I think it will be?'

'Have I got any evidence that my prediction is wrong or very unlikely to happen? Look at recent or past events when you have dreaded or predicted something bad would happen and it didn't, or if it did were you able to cope better than you thought you would?'

'So, should I still be thinking these things? What would a best friend tell me to think, what would I say to my best friend if she was thinking something bad was going to happen?'

'You need to stop rehearsing how to cope or behave in events that may or may not happen and stop having a post-mortem after events have occurred. The more you rehearse events before they happen, the more you will be focusing on the plan when you are at the event, so much so that you will probably not concentrate on the here and now. Then you are likely to feel nervous and make a mistake or not take in how well the event is actually going. After the event, if you start having a post-mortem of what you said, what you didn't say, who looked at you or who you heard laughing and looking at you; you will only probably remember negative things and become upset about them. You will probably forget and dismiss or play down the positive things.'

'Homework this week is therefore also going to be about catching yourself making negative predictions and challenging them, to not rehearse things and not post -mortem things, to notice when you are asking for reassurance and stop. Tell your family and friends to stop reassuring you. Also practice stopping avoidance, attack and passive behaviour. Remember to continue to practice mindfulness to help you deal with your emotions if you become distressed, or before anxiety provoking events.'On the way back home, the friends chatted about Claire potentially going to Syria in September with Karis and how Karis had given Claire an incentive to sort herself out. Claire had only self-harmed once recently and that was the night Karis had said she wanted to go with Claire. It meant, she had had the negative prediction that she would be let down, just as her mother had promised things and let her down.

'How are you and Tom doing?' Claire said while squinting, trying to drive with tired eyes.

'Yeah really good. It's just, well it just feels like...'

'It's going too quick or it's boring, oh I know it's not going to last?'

'It's not boring, I guess it just hasn't been a big romance thing. We are just comfortable together. It's not like we're kids though, is it?'

'You mean, you wanted to be pursued and thrown on the bed in a long white nightgown. Back to your historical novels again Dee.'

'I have never had that though Claire, you have. I feel like I have never had the big romance. Stupid I know.'

'It's not stupid, but the important thing is what happens after the pursuit isn't it. I do worry though about this obsession Tom's got about rescuing this child and everything. It seems a bit random, kind but random.'

'I suppose he's getting older and he's wanted a child for a while. I guess Abbie has brought this more into his mind.'

'What about you though Dee, are you really wanting to foster? You have never mentioned it before. I know you have wanted your own child and you've been thinking it won't ever happen.'

'I think I could love a child who wasn't mine. It's just, I wish we had had time alone first just me and Tom, but I guess the process could take months.'

'Does he want you to move in?'

'Yeah, he keeps mentioning it but with everything else going on with my job and this thing with Melissa.'

'Why do they mean you can't move in? You're not sure

about him, are you?'

'I am sure, he's amazing, he's caring, funny, hardworking. I think I just feel I have been here before and how do I know it will work this time?'

'Negative prediction! Can you challenge it with facts?'

'Well the facts are I have moved in with people twice before and it's gone horribly wrong.'

'This time it may be different though. He has no issues with alcohol, he doesn't control you; he's not a gambler. Come on Dee, maybe it's the real thing this time?'

'But what if it isn't?'

'Anyway, I'll see you sometime at work and we'll talk more then,' Claire lent across and pecked her on the cheek.

Dee's mum was waiting patiently to hear what had happened at the group. Dee walked into the kitchen and burst into tears.

'Mum, what if I get hurt again?'

'If you do, then we're here for you Dee and you'll dust yourself down and start out again like you've done before.' Dee's mum held her sobbing daughter and felt like crying herself.

'Dee, come on, here's your hot chocolate how about

you speak to Tom?' Dee's dad interrupted tentatively. He had developed a strong skill in knowing the right time to intervene. He did not show his emotions as much as his girls, but he felt them very keenly. He wanted his daughter to be happy, she deserved it. When Dee was happy then Shirley was also happy and that made his life much easier.

'Hi Tom,' Dee pretended to be chirpy as Tom's face appeared on her phone.

'You look upset. Tell me what's happened? Is it work or something at the group?'

'Everything I guess.'

'Talk to me, is it us?' Tom looked at her with an anxious expression. It seemed just like when he had spoken to his ex and he knew that, well that it was the end.

'I'm feeling frightened. I know we get on well, but I'm just frightened it will go wrong and everything.'

'Me too, I know what you mean but it does feel so right, and I have no doubts about you.'

'Yeah, but do you think you will get bored of me and well it will be difficult if we have a foster child then wouldn't it?'

'I'm not going to get bored of you Dee. Have I rushed things though, talking about fostering and everything? I'm sorry I've being stupid,' Tom looked at the floor.

'You're not stupid but the fostering idea seems a bit impulsive. I guess it will take months to get approved and everything won't it, so we need to make the most of our time alone together first, don't we?'

'I've been to Julia's tonight and found out about the process. It will take a good while. She doesn't think we could just ask for Abbie; we may be a match for another child instead. That was not really the purpose of it was it? I just liked the idea of keeping Abbie close to her brothers.'

'Are you going to apply then?'

'Well, I was thinking maybe we both need time to think more and I was wondering if you had come to a decision about whether you want to move in? Or perhaps I'm rushing you about that?'

'How about Saturday?' Dee teased.

'Really Dee, are you sure? When I said I loved you the other day you didn't reply.'

'I am totally in love with you Tom, just frightened of things going wrong. I will start packing a few bits to bring over from tomorrow and I'll go and tell mum and dad now.

'Dee, we will be right together you know.'

'I know.' she walked back downstairs just as her parents were retiring to bed. She announced she was moving out and they had a group hug.

Chapter 24

Wednesday morning at work, Dee overheard some staff talking in the staffroom about Mandy's baby shower on the Friday night. Dee hadn't been invited and she knew, rationally, why should she have been invited as she had only just arrived on the ward? But sadness overwhelmed her again. The outsider again. Just like at school.

Throughout the day it was hard to get it off her mind. Whenever she was near Mandy, she felt like dropping hints to see if she could get an invite but stopped short each time. She also noticed that the staff still went to Mandy for advice, even though she was often around and they could ask her. She felt, well, unwelcome.

She locked herself in the loo with her notepad and wrote the following down.

'People don't like me on the ward otherwise I would have been invited to Mandy's.'

'How can I challenge this - Mandy doesn't know me, probably not everyone has been invited. It's probably just people she is close to. She wouldn't have thought to invite me, it has probably been arranged for weeks. It doesn't mean she either does or doesn't like me. I am new to her. I want to subtly ask for reassurance she likes me, but that's the wrong thing to do.'

That night she met Tom at B and Q and chose some paint and furnishings for the bedroom and then they went for a meal. Dee told Tom about how easy it was for her to feel rejected and left out and again her regrets at taking the job.

'Look Dee, when you move in, well you don't even have to work if you don't want to, or if you want, you could just work part time; a couple of days or whatever. There's a nursing home ten minutes away. You can take it easier.'

'Thanks Tom but this is why I'm doing the self - esteem course isn't it, to fight the idea of not been good enough and not been liked. I have not been invited Friday as it was probably planned weeks ago, and they didn't know me then and have only just met me. It's not that they don't like me I guess they just don't know me. Next week Mandy won't be there, so they will have to ask me things then. I need to carry on with it, to try to improve my self-esteem.'

'Do you think you would want to work if we fostered?' Tom looked at her earnestly.

'Well, if I had a child then I'd definitely look to part time work or not working, depending on whether we could afford it and I had enough to do at home. Are you going to apply for fostering then?'

'I want to, but I just don't want to risk losing you. We are either both on board with it otherwise I won't do it.'

'I think we should try Tom,' they both smiled.

'What if we can't get Abbie though?'

'Then we will still have time to think what we want to do I guess?'

'What did your parents say about you moving in?'

'I think they think it may be a tad early, but they are happy we are getting on well. Sunday lunch is a permanent invite and I would still want to go visit them in the week one night after work.'

'Of course, since I lost my own mum; well it would be good to see your mum and I bet she'll be great with a grandchild. Your dad too.'

'Tell me about the application process then for fostering, is it horrendous?'

Dee listened while Tom explained. It was certainly thorough and daunting but not impossible. Tom explained that time was of the essence. Talking of Abbie, she was coming to Julia's for tea on Sunday so they would be able to see her again. Julia had offered to bring her round to see them.

Later, Tom and Dee snuggled up in bed together. It

was all about togetherness.. Things for once felt right.

Chapter 25

At Claire's home, she felt settled now that she had committed to the plan. She was going to Syria with the Red Cross in September. She had organized a career break for a year and had managed to get Karis a place to go with her. The two were now either chatting daily or seeing one another daily. As a result of the affection they both felt for one another, their mental health was beginning to improve. It was amazing what kindness and belonging could do for people feeling lost. They were able to be noticed and wanted and to have someone to care how each other was doing.

At Melissa's though things were still not right. Despite Geoff being in counselling he was now drinking to forget what the counselling had brought back up in his mind: the intrusive flashbacks of his dad hitting his mum, the guilt of not being powerful enough to stop it. Despite the counsellor reminding him that he had only been a weak child and it was never a child's responsibility to rescue a parent, somehow or other, he thought there was something he could have done. Just as he thought, deep down, there was something he could have spotted to prevent his client killing herself and her baby.

Melissa had moved into the spare bedroom now. He had let her, to her surprise. He did not want to risk more violence between them. He wanted to protect her from himself. It also allowed him more time for drinking alone from a hip flash he concealed in his bedside table, wrapped in his old scout shirt that he had kept as memorabilia. He was considering giving up the 'talking therapy' it seemed to be making him feel worse. He also wanted to give up the drinking and pledged to do so the next day.

Melissa was already fast asleep. It had been an exhausting couple of weeks. She had been busy sorting out what possessions to take when she left, what to get rid of and had been back and forth to the charity shop to donate stuff. She was almost there. Just the loft now. Mark would come tomorrow and help lift stuff down while Geoff was at work. She had some boxes of memorabilia that she would want to take with her. It was nearly time to go and she hadn't shed any tears. There was just an overwhelming relief and a steady rise of hope for her new future.

Chapter 26

On Saturday Dee had taken more clothes from her family home over to Tom's.

'We might need more storage?' Tom stood scratching his head at the volume of shoes that were arriving in the bedroom.

'Yep, I think so,' Dee started to look at the small space now left in the fitted wardrobe and the further suitcase she had to unload.

'I'll go put the kettle on,' Tom offered as if that was somehow going to solve everything.

Dee looked around the room. Although she felt comfortable in the house when Tom was there, on her own she felt uneasy. There was just something she couldn't put her finger on. A couple of times she had felt something behind her, a dark shadow or, well, she didn't know how to describe it. She had tried to tell Tom, but he just laughed. She asked the history of the house and whether he had had any similar experiences. Tom didn't believe in ghosts or 'any of that nonsense' as he described it. She had even woken in the night a couple of times, suddenly sensing movement in the room or creaks on the landing. She had lay awake at times trying to analyse the sounds. She would try to stir a snoring Tom to no avail. In her mind she supposed it was Tom's mum who was haunting the place or checking her out. Alone in the bedroom she began to feel on edge. Tom appeared with tea as she was busily distracting herself by unpacking.

'Tom, I've had that feeling again. You know, like what I told you about before...'

'I have lived here on my own since my mum died and have never felt anything or even previous to that. I think it's just you love; the stress of the new job is perhaps making you nervous. You will hear creaking noises in old houses, it's the wooden floors and when the central heating comes on,' he pulled her to him. They hugged and she felt safe. She always felt safe in his arms. His big muscular arms.

Sunday morning and Tom went to work. Dee got up and showered and decided, since it was a clear bright day, to go and explore the garden. She took a coffee out and a newspaper. The garden was sprouting new growths of perennials and was an abundance of activity. She sat at the bottom of the garden looking back at the house. She admired the winding path and the shaped borders; Tom's mum must have spent a lot of time there. The door- bell went.

There at the door stood Julia, with the twins in a double buggy. 'Hi, fancy a turn around the village. I'm just popping to the farm as we've run out of milk again.'

'Great, I'll just grab the keys to lock up.'

Dee was offered the pushchair to push. That was no mean feat. It was surprisingly heavy and unwieldy.

'Thanks for calling for me, I was just sitting in the garden admiring Tom's mum's handiwork.'

'Yeah, Bev was always gardening. They used to have an open garden for charity once a year. She loved to show it off.'

'Did you know Bev very well?'

'Not really, I tried to invite her round and she did come a couple of times, but she was a private person. I guess drinkers often are, they don't want you to see their habit.'

'Julia, do you think Tom and I stand a chance of getting Abbie?'

'I don't see why not; I have already tried to put a word in for you both with my support team.'

'You know if we did get Abbie would you give me advice and be there, because I don't have any notion of how to look after a young child?'

'Of course, you'll be great the two of you. Kids don't come with a manual. You will find your own ways...'

After the farm they called in the tiny shop, the one that sold everything. The shopkeeper, Joe, remembered Dee's name. She was beginning to feel accepted by the villagers whom her and Tom often bumped into. She was desperately trying to remember everybody's name. One person had even tried to talk to her about blood pressure problems. It seems having a general nurse in the village may be an asset, someone to call upon to give an enema, she surmised.

'I'll see you later then Dee, we'll bring Abbie round after tea.'

Julia left Dee at the garden gate and Dee suddenly felt bereft again. Julia was, well, Julia was like her mum, a comfort blanket. Back home she Facetimed her own mother. Dee told her again about the uneasy feelings she was getting, although that morning had been better. The house was lighter and she had kept the radio on. Dee's mum just thought it was about just getting used to the place and, like Tom, she did not believe in ghosts. She was pleased Julia had called but at the end of the conversation, Dee's mum felt a twinge of jealousy that Julia would probably see her daughter more than her. She would talk to Roy about arranging to visit Dee more often.

Tom arrived home to find the washing and ironing up to date and the online shopping had been done. Dee was a worker, unlike his ex.

They drove to Kate and Ben's, only ten miles away. Kate answered the door looking positively glowing. Kate, although pregnant, was still thinner than Dee and looked so healthy. She had a model like frame and her long black hair was scraped back in a ponytail.

'Come in you two.'

Ben was cooking lunch in the kitchen, so he welcomed Tom in to have a beer during the procedure, allowing Kate and Dee some girlie time.

'Kate, you look so well how's the morning sickness?'

'Okay now thank God. I think I have got past the worst of it. I'm feeling more like my usual self, other than I get tired more easily.'

'Are you still working fulltime?'

'Yeah, but I'm reducing my hours to three days a week in a couple of weeks and then I'll leave a month or so before baby is due. Do you want to see the nursery?' Kate grabbed Tom as well and they all went to have a look.

The room was painted white, but all the bedding and curtains were lime green polka dots and an orange carpet. It was bright and vibrant. Beautifully put together. A bit like Kate herself.

Tom was a practical type, worrying about the safety of a rug and electric sockets in the baby's room. He had, however, noticed Dee's face light up. He wanted them to have their own baby, he knew Dee would be a wonderful mother.

Downstairs Ben continued to talk about their plans to extend into the garden, The happy couple were infectious. All was good in their life. Everything was straightforward. They seemed to have no work stress, no money worries, no body image worries. How Dee would like the complete package. She would like to feel and look healthy. The dread of work then came over her in a wave. Back tomorrow and she did not want to go.

The two couples spent the afternoon talking about kids, holidays and DIY and at four o clock Dee and Tom left for home. Abbie would be coming soon.

At five o clock Abbie and Julia came around. Dee and Tom had set up a card making set on the table, thinking that Abbie may want to do another card to send to her mum. There was no dad involved anymore following his heroin overdose.

'What have you been doing at school this week?' Tom asked helping Abbie to sort out what she needed to make a card.

'I've done an Easter hat. I stuck chicks on it and pink ribbons.'

'Did you, and what kind of Easter egg would you like?' Tom was able to chat so naturally.

'Mini eggs, a big one.'

'Which colour mini egg do you like the best? I like the pink ones,' Dee asked trying to join in the conversation.

'I like the pink ones too.' Abbie turned and giggled

at Dee. It melted Dee's heart. She laughed back and they helped Abbie do a card, but she did not want to do it for her mum. It was for a secret person. She had drawn two eggs, stuck two yellow feathers on them and coloured them pink.

'This card is for you. Will you put it on the wall?' Abbie gave the card to Dee and hugged Tom.

Dee felt a lump in her throat and she could see that Tom was equally touched by the gesture..

'We'll put it on the fireplace and then we can see it every day,' Tom reshuffled some ornaments and propped the card up beside the clock.

'Can I live here with you?' Abbie asked Tom tugging at his jumper as she said it.

'Oh Abbie, that would be nice but if not, you can come to see us when you see your brothers.' Tom said it cheerfully, although obviously taken aback. Abbie reached her arms up wanting to be picked up. Julia looked over to Tom to give approval and Tom, swung the little girl up and into his arms. She clung to him and he caught her facial expression in the mirror. Her eyes were squeezed shut and she was smiling. Dee looked on, partly jealous that Abbie hadn't wanted her to pick her up but mainly in admiration of Tom. He was a good man. Her man.

'Where would I sleep?' now Abbie turned to Dee.

At this point Julia interjected, 'Abbie, we need to get

going you have school tomorrow and it's getting late.'

Abbie started crying and protesting she didn't want to go. The crying turned into a tantrum. Julia moved in to calm her and so the visit ended abruptly with Julia ushering Abbie out. She tried to distract her by suggesting that she could see the twins and play a few more minutes before she had to be picked up. It left Dee and Tom feeling bereft.

'I bet they won't allow us to see her again. They'll say it's affecting her, won't they?' Tom turned to Dee in desperate need of reassurance.

'I hope they don't stop her seeing us but next time it may be best to see her at Julia's. Look at the positives though, she likes us.'

That night Julia and Patrick sat contemplating what else they could do to help Tom and Dee become approved as foster parents to get Abbie. Julia would talk to the team tomorrow to see if they could speed up their application process.

After checking with Julia how Abbie was when she left to go back home, Dee and Tom sat all night thinking about Abbie.

'I feel bad Dee, we have perhaps given her false hope. I feel we have done a bad thing,' They sat hugging one another.

'I know and now if we can't get her, it will confuse her, and she will feel let down by people again. Just like her mum let her down,' Dee sniffled.

'When I was holding her Dee, it felt so good. I was so happy and now...' Tom was feeling defeated.

'Come on, like Julia says look at the positives. She likes us. Why don't you chase up the application tomorrow?'

Chapter 27

At Claire's, things had seemingly been going okay until her mother had started to act up. The news of Claire going to work abroad seemed to have made her want to drink and then threaten to kill herself. It had all been a puzzle to Claire who always believed her mum wouldn't care whether she lived or died. It seemed another way for her mum to gain attention from others. A kind of 'woe is me my daughter is going to work abroad and leave me.' She had started to call Claire more often at night, often intoxicated, suggesting her life was not worth living and she felt like overdosing.

Claire being a nurse went through the motions of offering a shoulder to cry on and reassuring her mother things would be okay, but deep down she felt bitter, resentful and confused. She often had the nagging image of finding her mum dead and not feeling upset. This in turn upset and confused her. How could she feel this way now, when all her life she had wanted to feel significant to her mum. Now she was it didn't seem to matter?

Claire's mum had also done her best to denigrate Karis, suggesting she was a leech and should look to her own mother rather than Claire. Many times, Claire just hung up the phone as she couldn't stand her mum's toxicity any longer. Claire also had second thoughts at times about going abroad, having fantasies of rekindling a relationship with her mum and doing girlie shopping with her just like Dee and Shirley. Then she reminded herself it would never be. She could see through her mum. Her mum just didn't want her to be happy. She wanted her daughter to stay miserable just as she had been all through her life. Claire tossed it around so many times in her mind. She was unperturbed by family alerting her to her mum's welfare and she was determined to go to Syria. She would do this for herself and Karis. She would be the motherly figure to Karis and help turn the young girl's life around, in turn she would be changing her own life?

Another Sunday night and Geoff sat with the kids, his mind already dreading work the following day. Melissa had some choir practice at the church, and he had been left babysitting. The kids were now in bed and he was just alone with his hipflask. Just one before bed to help him sleep would not hurt...

Chapter 28

Monday morning and Dee's dream job seemed insignificant now. Her only thoughts were of Abbie and the little girl's scrunched up face and sobbing the day before.

She started looking at doing the staff rota and other admin but Dee's mind just was not there. She tried to stay focused, but it was difficult. Even a relative shouting at her that her mother's bed was soiled, seemed to pass over her head. Dee didn't want to be there. She wanted to be back at the cottage making it a home, maybe for Abbie. She had to get Abbie and bring her home.

Tom had phoned the fostering company at nine am. They were going to try to fast track the fostering process. They would start the ball rolling getting references for them and criminal record checks etc. At the beginning of June there was a four-day information and training course that they had been booked on. It could however take up to October to get final approval. The company was the same one who fostered Abbie and had already been tipped off by Julia that the couple were keen to offer Abbie a long-term foster placement.They were, therefore, eager to process the application, as quickly as possible.

Over lunch, Dee received a text re the status of the application and she booked the time off work. Was this really happening, would they be approved? They had only been together a few weeks after all. Dee felt a surge of excitement. Was she really going to be a mother and have a normal life? Was it her time to shine, not at work but at home? Work was immaterial now. Being a manager did not appear to be what she thought it would be. She would let Claire know in the next month or so to look for someone else to do the job. Dee had lost all interest in it.

She was even tempted to tell Claire to stuff the job on the way to the course on Tuesday night, but instead bit her tongue. Claire was so busy telling her about her mother's behaviour, that Dee didn't want to give her any more bad news.

'Are you still going to Syria then?' Dee enquired.

'Yep, she's not going to stop me. She is using this to enhance her victim status, that's all. She just doesn't want me to be happy.'

'What do you mean victim status?'

'You know over the years she's moaned on about how she was used and thrown away by her boyfriend and how he tricked her into letting me move out. How awful it was that she was forced to live without her daughter and that now her daughter has chosen to go abroad and leave her?'

'I don't know what to say Claire, other than I'm sorry

she's not supporting you. It seems selfish.'

'Toxic you mean. Anyway, what's your news, how's the ward?'

'Not what I thought it would be I guess.'

'You thought everyone would show you respect, and they don't or what do you mean?'

'All the admin and management bits. I didn't realize how much there was to the job and you know I'm a dinosaur when it comes to IT.'

'You will get used to it.'

'Tom and I are doing well, and the fostering process is starting to go through. I'll need a week off beginning of June to do a course.'

'Dee are you really sure? You've just got your management job and everything, why don't you give it longer? It'll be difficult to get part time hours as a manager you know.'

'I know, I'll give up altogether probably.'

'Give up nursing, you can't be serious?'

'Deadly serious. I want a different life, Claire. Don't you?'

'I don't know what I want yet, but hopefully Syria will clarify that.'

The confidence building group had dwindled to only

three out of the original fifteen clients. Joy stood at the front of the room and welcomed them.

'So homework. How did we all do?'

Dee reported her success on not seeking reassurance about not been invited to Mandy's baby shower. The group praised her and shared some of their own homework results about how they challenged negative predictions.

Claire had spoken about beginning to trust Karis to be a genuine person who would remain in her life and as a result Claire was no longer avoiding her. She was trying to work on her rule for living, which was people cannot be trusted, so avoid getting too close.

'Right, this week we are discussing how self -critical we are when we have poor self-esteem. How we can chastise ourselves, berate ourselves and punish ourselves at times for perceived faults or wrong doings. Often, we have been doing this for years. We need to ask ourselves; does it help?

'Often the things we criticize ourselves for, may be based on the irrational belief that we did something wrong. Often, we criticize ourselves for things we did as children, when our mind was not yet mature, and we were perhaps following the crowd. Maybe there may be some truth in what we are saying to ourselves. We may not be as academically bright as others, as beautiful as others etc. but does that mean we deserve to punish ourselves? Think of your attributes, skills and achievements in life. Think of the compliments or kindness others show to you.'

Claire reflected in front of the group, 'Dee can be awfully hard on herself and forget what she has done well. She just focuses on the mistakes.'

'That's exactly right Claire, people with low self-esteem are like blinkered shire - horses. They zone in on the memories of mistakes and guilt and forget achievements and positive attributes. Then on a daily basis you all have heightened awareness of looking out for things you have done wrong and forgetting the good things you have done. You will look for incidents when you perceive disapproval or rejection from others and dismiss validation and belonging from others.'

The group all seemed to relate to this, and Dee started to think about the replay of Abbie's visit and how she had dwelt on Abbie getting upset at the end and not all the good bits in between.

'Then you all put yourselves down or encourage others to criticize you. 'I am such an idiot, I made a fool of myself like always, I never get it right'. You all need to be kinder to yourselves. Here's how.' Joy went back to the whiteboard and wrote:

'What am I saying to myself?'

'What factual evidence have I got that what I am saying is correct?'

'What contradictory evidence have I got that it isn't

true?'

'If my best friend had criticised themself, how would I ask them to challenge this?'

'So, what should I be saying to myself? Maybe something like: 'I didn't handle it well today but, in the past, I have handled situations like this well and I can do so again. I am not an idiot; everyone gets things wrong sometimes. Everyone gets laughed at sometimes.'

The group lapped it all up. It made sense to everyone and when they left the meeting that night, they did so with determination to use the thought challenging technique in the future. They felt armed to help themselves. The trick was to remember the techniques. It was so easy to slip into old ways.

Dee dropped in to see her parents on the way back. She filled them in with what had happened with Abbie and they both looked concerned. Dee sensed that they were not fully behind the idea of the fostering and knew they were just worried whether she and Tom would make it or whether she would just get hurt again. She knew all that, but she still wanted them to be on board. She decided to reflect it back to them. Afterwards for once it was her dad who took the lead.

'Dee, you know we will support you with Abbie whether you get her or not and with either a foster child or with your own child. In fact, I've already started a woodworking project for a child's bedroom. We are also excited about being grandparents and your mum has actually been thinking of retiring.'

'Yes darling, we just worry that you may get your hopes up, but we are praying for you that it all works out. Would it be possible for us to meet Abbie?'

'I'd love you to, but I doubt whether we will be able to see her again for a while now, after what happened. I love you both so much and I hope it happens for all of us. Tom has said I can give up work then if I want to and we can all spend more time together.'

'You mustn't give up your job Dee, I can look after a child for you while you work,' Dee's mum frowned and bit her nails.

'Mum, don't you see; I want to be a homemaker. We have no mortgage and Tom has got his inheritance; I can always return in the future if I really needed to.'

Her mum looked over to her husband for support, but he stayed quiet. Secretly although proud that his daughter was a nurse, he did not like what the job did to her emotionally and physically. He hated the verbal abuse she had to take from the public and worried about her driving home when she was tired. They had a group hug and arranged to meet on the Sunday at the cottage to go to the village pub for a meal.

Driving home Dee felt more positive. She fantasised about her parents playing with Abbie in the cottage garden, while she and Tom did a barbecue. Julia and Patrick would be there and the twins. Kate and Ben would be there with the new baby. It would be like a village scene from a Jane Austen novel, a gathering of loved ones. A happy day.

Back home Tom was already in bed reading the paper. She snuggled in next to him and told him about the night. Every time he noticed her criticising herself or putting herself down, he was to say, 'Dee remember what you have got to do?'

'Have you booked the time off work for the course?' he patted her hand.

'Yep, I've told Claire as well. She intimated how hard it would be to go part time as a manager, but I said I would probably leave at that point anyway.'

'I have been thinking. You could leave now if you want to. Then we can focus on getting the house ready and you can get used to not working and everything. We need to finish the bedroom and I was considering whether we should get the builder in for a quote to knock the kitchen through. It would be easier to have a kitchen like Kate's having so if we were in the kitchen a child can be sat at the table playing or doing homework or whatever.'

'I guess it's frightening, the idea of giving up nursing completely, but I don't think I will miss the job. I would just worry if we didn't make it. I would have no income. I love the idea of a kitchen diner though.'

'Dee, we are going to make it; if I wasn't sure I wouldn't be going down the fostering route. You are my soulmate. But are you having doubts?'

'Definitely, I still have the nagging doubt that you're not real.'

'Does this feel real?' Tom pulled her toward him and their naked bodies met Dee giggled as he rolled on top of her.

Chapter 29

On Thursday night Dee met Melissa at her local pub for a meal. Dee watched her arrive, late as always looking pale and baggy eyed. They hugged as they met.

'Have you changed your mind, Mel?'

'Well, I may have the salmon and not the chicken,' her eyebrows raised. She shifted in her seat and Dee knew that Melissa would prefer not to get a lecture. She carried on to say, 'Okay, so can I know when and where yet?'

'It will be soon but that's all I can say.'

'Have you told your parents Mel?'

'Don't be stupid, you know they'll tip Geoff off. They will be the last to know where I am. I don't think Geoff suspects anything. He made some comment the other day about an ornament not being in the lounge, but I said I was having a change around and was working on a mood board. He hasn't noticed the kid's wardrobes are about empty, I'm just keeping four days of clothes in there so I can throw them in a suitcase on the day.'

'How do you think Geoff will really react? Do you think he will get depressed?'

'He will probably drink more and feel sorry for himself; I'm just hoping this will get him to go for help. He can visit the kids in the summer then. Mark has already sorted out a friend who can give him a room for a few days. Then he can take the kids out in the daytime. There's a beach up the road.'

'How're things with you and Mark?' Dee daren't meet Mel's eyes.

'We had sex in the churchyard the other day, it was great.'

'Oh no Mel, what if anyone had seen you?' she then saw Mel sniggering. and realised she was joking.

'I don't know if there's anything there or not, I get mixed messages. The more we talk, the more we have in common and he talks about long term plans like doing a mission placement in Africa and all kind of things. I could go with him. When I try and look flirty, he just backs off. So, I don't know, but I hope in the future maybe there could be something. Who'd have thought I'd fancy a vicar?'

That made them both giggle. Then Dee told her the news about Abbie and work.

'I can't believe after all these unhappy years that in the same year things are going to change for the better for both of us. It's plain weird,' Melissa grabbed Dee's hand. They looked at one another.

'It's just a shame, we won't be able to meet so much though, Mel. I don't know how I will cope with you wherever and Claire in Syria.'

'You have new friends now don't forget. We'll Facetime every week and I will only be less than three hours away. So you can come for weekends. You will love it there. It's beautiful countryside but it's close to the coast as well.'

'Won't you feel guilty for leaving Geoff though, Mel? I still feel sorry for him, and he hasn't got any close family, has he? Has he got a lot of friends?'

Mel glanced down and said quickly, Oh I think it'll be okay. He's got a couple of good friends from work and they're social workers don't forget. They will rally round him. I'm sure that Alice from work has always had a bit of a thing for him. Before I arrived on the scene, I think they'd got close and she was divorced last year. I don't think he'll be on his own for long. He will be able to read in peace and quiet as well. I think it will suit him not having the kids around. He still has hardly anything to do with them.'

When Dee got home, Tom was still out at a social function with work. He had asked Dee to go but she had declined as she knew it would often be a late night with a lock in. He had left the hallway light on for her, but it was still a tad spooky going into the house alone. She still felt uneasy. She avoided being in the house alone and despite Tom's reassurances about the history of the place she had considered asking Mark the vicar to pop around and bless it.

Dee very much believed in ghosts. She had felt plenty of uneasiness working on the hospital wards and walking along the long corridors especially at night. She would gaze out of the dark windows and imagine faces staring back. Mog greeted her which was a welcome distraction and she headed up the stairs to the bathroom. Tom's mum's bedroom door was left ajar so that the paint could still dry and so that the room felt part of the house again. After her death Tom had closed it out of emotional pain.

She quickly showered and slid into bed. She grabbed a book and within a few minutes she was snoozing. She didn't even hear Tom slam the door shut and flush the loo. He had left long before everyone else. He was always eager to get home to his Dee.

On the Sunday they both got up early as Dee was volunteering that day. Kate joined her. The two chatted idly and swapped building tips so that Dee could contact the builder about the kitchen. Dee told Kate all about Mel's situation and Claire and by the end of the tale; Kate felt as though she too knew the other women. To Kate who was always highly pragmatic it sounded like a TV soap opera. She said that she was glad she lived her straightforward life with Ben. Her only worry now was not gaining too much weight; Kate had never been able to pinch more than an inch.

Chapter 30

Tom had bumped into Julia who had had good news about Abbie. She was visiting again on Sunday and she asked if they could join Tom and Dee for lunch at the pub? Neutral ground might be good for Abbie, so she felt less attached to the idea of moving in with Dee and Tom and just recognized them as friends. The foster parent Sue would leave Abbie in Julia's care for the afternoon.

Julia, Patrick, the twins and Abbie were waiting at the pub when Dee, her parents and Tom got there.

Julia and Dee's mum hit it off straight away, but everyone focused their attention on Abbie. Dee's parents talked to her non-stop and Dee and Tom barely got a look in. Abbie sat at the table with Julia but sidled in-between Tom and Dee at one point. She was eager to tell them about going to her friends for tea. She didn't stop chattering. She happily pulled herself onto Tom's knee. Tom looked to Julia for reassurance that this was alright, but Julia just smiled and laughed.

Dee noticed that her mum kept looking at her. She was aware that she looked happier than she had for a long time. Abbie smiled at Dee. They looked like a family. Shirley gave her daughter an encouraging smile. Dee's dad was watching benevolently.

'Why don't we all go back to mine for a coffee?' Julia invited everyone.

Back at Julia's the twins frolicked on the floor with their toys and Abbie played with them while the adults looked on. Julia was busy discussing cooking recipes with Dee's mum and Patrick and her dad discussed sport. Tom and Dee crawled around on the floor interacting with all the kids. They managed to have a game of pairs with Abbie on their own and noticed how bright she was. She was contented today and didn't ask again about living with them or anything, but when it was time to go, she asked if she would see them again next week. They replied, 'It will be soon.'

Later back at the cottage, Dee's dad said, 'She's great. Abbie's very bright isn't she Shirl?'

'She sure is but we would need to do something with her hair perhaps plait it, as it's straggly, bless her. We can sort that out. She's well behaved.' She grabbed her daughter's hand. 'What do you think the chances are that you'll get her?'

'Well I don't see why we won't pass the feasibility test and interviews, what may go against us is how long we've been together. If not, I could try to just foster in my name. I am hoping it won't be a problem though,' Tom said brightly.

'Let's go and look at the kitchen then, if you want me to draw some plans up,' Dee's dad said making his way through to the kitchen.

After Dee's parents had left the couple opened a bottle of red and sat by the fire.

'Tom, I was thinking about what you said about me giving up work and, well, we have never really discussed money and logistics before. Is it ok for you to tell me how we will manage on just your wage?'

'Course, I told you I had an inheritance from my dad when he passed over. My dad's family are very wealthy. Then of course mum died, and she was insured. Would you be shocked if I said I have a million in the bank and we live in a small cottage and I work as an estates manager?'

'A little puzzled I guess, but that's what I like about you Tom; you're not pretentious in any way and you just want to live a simple wholesome life.'

'Yeah, the interest and other investments I have plus my wage are more than enough to keep a family. I would love for you to have the choice of being a stay-at-home mum, but if you still want to work; I am sure Julia or Shirley will help us out with childcare. It is up to you Dee. Please don't go telling everyone about the money though.'

'No, I won't say anything, I'll just tell my parents, so they don't worry about us. I will make my mind up about work at some point.'

'Are you going to ring the builder then and start

getting some quotes? Dad said he would draw the plans up for building regulations. He didn't seem to think it would cost too much, especially because he will do bits himself as well. I think he'd like that.'

'Yep. There is a builder who lives locally. I'll phone him. Can you choose the bedding and curtains for the bedroom then?'

'Well, if we look for the bed online it might be nice for me and mum to look for bedding and pictures and bits. She would like that.'

'

The next day at work was non-stop. A constant queue of people appearing at the office door. 'Sorry to bother you, there is a relative who just wants a quick word.'

By the end of the day, she had left half an hour late and her head was spinning.

She had, however, had chance to take in the atmosphere between Sam and Sophie. Sam was pulling faces at Sophie when she was handing over patients to the late staff and giggling at her when she walked past. She was encouraging the housekeeper to do the same. Sophie must have noticed the jeering. She looked a sad and a lonely figure. Dee again tried to invite her into the office for a chat, but again she declined. She wrote down what she had witnessed that day. That was it -she would keep a diary. She would get Sam. If it were the last and only achievement she made as a manager she would catch a bully.

In the two weeks that followed, she took every opportunity she could get to listen out for Sam's interactions with Sophie and write things down. Then she would present the information to Claire to see what could be done. Dee was also watching Nina to record her sickness and leaving early to go home.

Dee felt a lonely figure. Other than her daily interactions with Maureen, the ward clerk, she never seemingly had meaningful, personable interactions with anyone. It had, however, become more bearable to know that by the end of the year she was hoping to not be there anymore, or possibly sooner. Then she could fantasize about putting two fingers up to Sam. She couldn't have stopped herself being bullied and left out at school, but she was determined to try to help Sophie at work.

At the self-esteem group they had moved onto session six and session seven. Session six had been about being more accepting of yourself and remembering the achievements and attributes you had. Dee had found this difficult to write down. She was so dismissive of her qualities and achievements. She was, however, able to acknowledge that she was hardworking and caring and now she could say she had achieved being a manager, even though she was not enjoying it. She had stuck her achievements and attributes on the fridge door and reminded herself of them every day before going to work. Tom would always scribble more on, such as 'bakes great scones' or 'flexible in bed'...

Session seven had been about adjusting your rules of living. Dee's rule was "I must be good at my job, otherwise

I will feel inadequate.' Dee's new rule became, 'no one is good at their job all the time. I will aim for 70 percent good. I can achieve 70 percent good enough and this will still be a lot higher than most other people's levels.'

The other rule of living Dee tried to adjust was 'I must be liked and be accepted. I must fit in.' She tried to adjust it to, 'I can't always be liked in the same way I don't always like others. It doesn't mean I am a bad person. I have made new friends though recently and they seem to like me and I have a new partner who loves me.'

It was still difficult for her though when she didn't feel liked or she felt left out at work. She sensed the staff chit chatting about her when they walked past her office, probably wondering if she was skiving. They didn't know the huge volume of admin. work she had to do. Unless they saw her out on the ward doing practical things, they thought she was a waste of space. She did, of course, do as much as she could to go out and lend a hand and always offered to do at least one round of drinks a day. She concluded in the end that it would never be enough. They would never think she justified the extra £100 a month she got for being a manager. She even reflected that now she was not doing shifts she was about on the same money as before. Dee had accepted that it would probably take another year at least to be accepted and recognized as a manager. They just saw her as a fill-in. Mandy was their manager. If it had not of been for Tom and Julia, she would have felt hurt by their rejection, but she just accepted it. As for changing her rule of living about being good at her job, she just tried to aim for seventy percent effort. She hadn't even got reports done on time and risked the wrath of Claire as a result. She was not prepared to knock herself out now for a job. She had to keep herself well for the fostering application.

Chapter 31

Claire had embraced the changes in rules for living. She had stopped believing she had to please her mum and family to be accepted as been good enough. Now when her mum phoned, she would often let it go to voicemail. She wasn't afraid to speak her mind to her mum. She had even come out with it and called her mum a victim and accused her of abandoning her when she was young. She told her about the damage it had caused her. Her mother had heard it all before but seemed to be grasping it more now, even tentatively apologizing at times.

Geoff arrived home on Friday the 1st of April with a sense of calm, more than usual. He had had a good week at work. A child protection conference had resulted in a vulnerable child going into permanent care so he would no longer have to worry about them. As he drove to the house, he saw the lounge in darkness. Perhaps Mel had taken the kids to the play barn. It meant he could chill for an hour or so till they got back. He walked round the back as usual to the kitchen and found the light on and a casserole cooking. It smelt good. By the kettle was an envelope.

'Dear Geoff

I am sorry but I have gone away. As you must know things have not been well with us for an awfully long time have they? I think it is best that we separate, but you can still see the kids and you can keep your house as I have somewhere to stay. I am not going to be local but have got a job as a live-in housekeeper up North. I will phone you Saturday night and the kids can speak to you as well and we can talk about when you can see them next.

I know this is hurtful Geoff, but I couldn't see another way and we couldn't continue the way we were, as it's no good for any of us. I will phone you tomorrow.

Mel

PS I have put a sausage casserole on for you.

Geoff slumped down on the kitchen chair and felt numb. He kept reading the letter over and over as if it were going to say something different the next time. He felt his throat tighten and tears stung his eyes. He lunged for his mobile, but Mel's phone was switched off. He left pleading voicemails and texts, begging her to come home so they could talk things through. He phoned her parents and they professed to know nothing about any of it and said they would try to contact her.

He stood up despairingly, letting the letter drift to the floor. 'But there was a love surely,' he said out loud.

He reached into the oven as though rescuing himself from a loveless vacuum. He slid the dish out and held it in his hands and stared into the simmering brew as if her love would reach out to him. The casserole dish was scalding hot and burnt his hands. He dropped it. The white floor tiles were splattered with fiery sausages and thousands of shards of ovenware. He felt the hope leave his body and rage take over.

He headed for the shed and his secret stash of Johnny Walker finest.

'Of course, Dee would know where she was.' He would ring Dee.

There was no answer from Dee's phone. 'That was it they were in it together, they had planned it, coerced and made me; made me an April Fool'. Geoff sat working it out in his mind, piecing things together. The choir practice, the girlie catch up with Dee. He sat on the tatty deckchair and sipped his whisky, peering out into the garden. It was drizzling now and dark. He took in the familiar smell of old paint tins and creosote. He looked round at the sawdust on the floor and the dusty shelves. He thought about the scores of jobs he wanted to do, the ones he had made half promises to complete but never did.

From the small gap in the grimy window, he could see the apple tree glistening with a smothering of fairy lights. He tried Dee once more.

'Dee as soon as you get this can you come to see me; I could do with some support. Mel's gone. I am guessing you knew all about this.' The screen blackened and died.

Hope had finally slipped through his burnt fingers and reality kicked in, as much as the whisky had taken hold. He sat a while longer holding his phone and staring at the tree, 'April Fool' ringing through his head. The voice seemed to sound like his father's mocking him as he did as a child. 'Mummy's boy, where's your mother? In bed for a change.' He swigged another whisky.

He wrapped himself in a blanket he and Mel shared picnics on when they had first met. It wasn't big enough now for the four of them to sit on. They were happy times of frolicking in sand dunes. 'How quickly things had changed.' He thought about signs of change he had tried desperately to ignore. How she would turn her back on him in bed and face the other way. He studied the apple tree. Mel always said the tree would grow bigger and stronger; like them as a couple.

Geoff staggered to his feet and started to pace around the shed, his eyes darting from one object to another. The damp and cold were biting into his flesh now, his bones ached and his eyes felt heavy. Anger raged inside, born from hunger and exhaustion. 'How did I end up in a life as pathetic as my mother and father?' He felt he had become an object of ridicule at home and work. He used to be a person that Mel and his colleagues looked up to. 'Now I am poor old Geoff, no wife and no pride.' Then it suddenly became clear what he should do...

Dee was washing the dishes at her parents house after they had Friday fish and chips with them. She had left her phone in her coat pocket. She checked it to see if Claire had texted about them meeting the following day. She then saw the missed call from Geoff. She listened to the bitterness and angst in his voice. It was now eight thirty. She stood frozen. 'This was it then Mel had gone...'

It was nine pm when Tom and Dee had arrived at Geoff's house. There was no lounge light on.

'They don't use the front door, we will have to go around the back,' Dee held Tom's hand.

'Look Dee, if he is pissed then we will just leave him and offer to come again tomorrow. If he starts to get nasty, we will leave as well. You know nothing anyway. Has Mel not answered your call yet?'

Dee checked her phone. No texts from Mel. As they went around the back the kitchen light was on and the door was wide open.

'Geoff.' Dee shouted outside the door not wanting to intrude.

'Dee, listen to me carefully go back to the car and phone an ambulance. Don't turn around just let me take you and point you in the right direction.' Tom endeavored to protect her, but it was too late. Dee swung round and there swaying gently from the apple tree, lit up slightly by the glow of the fairy lights, was Geoff.

'Ring an ambulance, Dee.' Tom picked up the step ladders from the floor and reached inside his coat secret pocket for his army knife; to cut the noose. Dee was frozen to the spot. All her years of being a nurse and there she was in a state of shock. Tom grabbed the phone from her and phoned while desperately trying to cut Geoff down.

'Dee please, he's still warm, come on we need to try to

resuscitate him.'

Dee suddenly came to her senses and rushed over to try compressions. She tried mouth-to-mouth but she knew it was futile. His neck was broken, his face was pale and his eyes bloodshot. It was only ten minutes before the ambulance arrived, but it seemed forever. They knew his neck was broken and told Dee to stop. Geoff had gone.

It was all a blur from that point on. The police had arrived and taken statements from Tom and tried to from Dee. Tom had shown the police her phone and they tried to phone Mel and left messages for her to phone them urgently. Tom had told them the tale of Mel planning to leave and why. The police searched the house for a suicide note. Dee sat oblivious, staring at the apple tree and still seeing Geoff there. She had been wrapped in a heat blanket. The ambulance crew had checked her over and thought she was in shock. She had to drink sweet tea and put her head between her knees. She dare not close her eyes for fear of what she would see. She felt terrible guilt. Geoff had phoned her at seven. He was alive then. If she had only answered her phone, he may still be alive. It was her fault. She should have told him Mel's plans. Now look what had happened. She was just as guilty as Mel. She and Mel had been responsible for Geoff's death.

'What about the children?' Tears ran down Dee's face. The police had been satisfied that there were no further questions for them now. Still there may be going forward but for now they could go home.

'Do you want me to take you to your mum's Dee?' Tom led Dee back to the car like she was a small child.

'Yes, I want my mum and dad,' Dee sobbed hysterically and garbled on about being guilty and the ifs and buts. Tom tried to reassure her none of this was her fault, but she was fixated on her part in it. A little way into the journey she threw up and felt like she was going to faint. Tom did an emergency stop and despite being covered in sick held her and cried himself. He too was pretty shaken by the whole experience.

Dee's mum threw the door open, grabbed hold of her daughter and ushered her to her annex. She showered and put her into bed like she was five. Dee just sobbed. Her dad made them all drinks and gave Tom a stiff whisky. He sat Tom down and warned him that things would be difficult for a while and to be patient with Dee. His daughter was not as resilient as she looked. Tom instinctively seemed to sense that. In fact, it was Dee's emotional vulnerability that appealed to him. He was determined to be her rescuer in life. They slept at her parents' home that night.

Dee tossed and turned and then at seven am, the phone went and a distraught Mel was on the line. Tom intercepted the call and spoke to her. The police had already done so. Dee was still sleeping and so he said he would get her to phone Mel later. Dee had kept waking throughout the night with nightmares, a faceless person coming toward her; a bright light and then nothing. She would wake up shouting out 'No, no' and Tom would gently whisper 'it's alright, it's just a dream.' Then Dee would drift off again.

Tom although shattered had been awake since five.

He had had to cancel his work. He lay thinking about how he could best support Dee, but also fearing how this may affect their chances of fostering. Mental health was assessed as well as stability and present home situation. Would they suggest that they wait a while with all the recent upset? Tom rolled onto his side and looked at Dee. Poor Dee, she didn't deserve this, and he felt bitter toward Mel for her actions involving Dee in it. She had involved him as well. It was not a scene that would be easy for him to forget. Dee woke up suddenly and felt confused as to why they were in her old bedroom and then it hit her and the tears came again. Her mum overheard her daughter.

'I've got a pot of tea and toast for you here, can I come in?'

Tom got up and headed for the bathroom leaving Dee and her mum together. 'She should never have involved you in this Dee. It's so unfair that this has happened to you. You wait till I see her next. You have always had to bail her out. Well she has done it this time. Those poor children, no dad now.'

'Shirley don't talk like that. It's not helping.' Dee's dad shouted outside the bedroom door.

'I should have hinted to him, I should have done something; I should have been there for him,' Dee cried unable to catch her breath. Her phone started to ring. It was Claire trying to organize a time to meet.

'Claire, something terrible has happened...'

Within a couple of hours Claire was round, trying to talk sense into Dee as she had always had to over the years. It seemed to help calm her but then the phone went again and it was Mel. Claire took over the call as soon as Dee said who it was. She calmly took the phone out of the bedroom and spoke to Mel alone.

When Dee asked how Mel was, she was told she was obviously upset and would call later and Mel was sorry that Dee had had to find Geoff.

The whole group sat together in the bedroom trying to talk about everything apart from what had just happened. They drank lots of tea. Dee started to feel sick again and a headache had come. Her mum dosed her up on paracetamol and suggested she had a sleep and that they needed to leave her alone. At the thought of being left alone, she clung to Tom and asked him not to leave her. Her eyes were heavy and yet she was afraid to close them in case the strange figure came again. When she woke in an hour, her mum ran her a bath and Tom suggested they all went back to the cottage as Mog would need feeding and, he said that although he had a cat - flap he would be wondering where they were. Dee however didn't want to go. She wanted to stay in her bed a while longer and said that she would come later.

As Tom drove home, a fear went through his mind.

'Would Dee come back?'

It was four in the afternoon. Dee and her mum were lying under the duvet together. Mel had phoned but Dee couldn't face speaking to her and left her dad to take the call. She would of course speak as soon as she was able to. Her mum was doing her best to distract Dee, talking about the cottage and their plans for the kitchen. Dee was faraway. She felt numb. It was as if her body were there, but her mind wasn't. Whatever they talked about, watched on the TV, or saw in a magazine seemed to somehow have links to Geoff and suicide. There was no doubt she was in shock still. She had, of course. seen many terrible things over the years both while training as a nurse and being qualified. She had seen people decapitated, burnt beyond all recognition, mauled by dogs but she had never seen anyone close to her dead. When her grandparents had died, she didn't want to see them at the morgue. She had of course seen her pet dog Timmy dead. In fact, she found him in the morning when she had gone to stroke him; all stiff and lifeless.

Tom had phoned but Dee had persuaded her mum to say she would phone him later. She needed to get rid of her headache first. Unfortunately, it was nearly ten at night and the headache had got worse. She would need to stay the night and try to get back to Tom's in the morning. She phoned Tom who had already assumed this would be the case. Although feeling hurt that she had retreated to her parents he tried to show understanding, reminding her that Abbie would be at Julia's the following day again. The plan was to go to the park if the weather was good. He thought this would cheer Dee up, but it seemed to have the opposite effect and she started to cry. There were now two more children in the world without a father and she could have done something to prevent it. She was the definition of a truly bad person.

At the vicarage it had also been a day full of tears and blame. Mark, the vicar, had spent his first day in his new job trying desperately to console Mel. Like Dee, she had taken to her bed and not only was Mark trying to fuss over her but look after the two kids who were oblivious to the scene. They were just eager to explore their new home and garden. Running around from one room to the next, asking questions and creating lots of laughter.

Mel was in shock. 'Why would he have done this?' She hugged her kids and felt sad they would not have him around in their life. 'Why would he have given up on them? He had so much to still live for...'

Mark had tried to listen and reassure her that although it was tragic, she was not to blame. It fell on deaf ears though. Mel knew in her heart she was to blame. She had killed Geoff.

She had a flashback of when she was sixteen and her parents told her that she had ruined their family life with her behaviour. 'You're a selfish girl, it's all about you.' They were right, she had been selfish and now look what had happened.

At Dee's parents it was midnight and Dee suddenly felt alone and frightened despite her mother sharing the bed with her, but now her mum was fast off.

Twice Dee had started to nod off and the face had jolted her awake again. She switched the lamp on and started to read, then she began to worry that if she couldn't cope with things like this, then how would she cope with Abbie. Poor Tom, first he has an alcoholic mother to care for and now a histrionic partner. The tears came again even though she was reading a Sophie Kinsella, she just could not raise a smile.

When she woke at seven on the Sunday morning, her mum had already left the room. She snuggled under her duvet and tried to read again. She ignored her phone and it occurred to her that she had best not go to work that week, she needed time to get over this. She would need to phone Mel., She couldn't keep avoiding her; it was her duty as a best friend. Mel was the chief mourner so why was Dee making a scene. She needed to get back to the cottage as well. Purposefully, she slipped out of bed and went to the shower room. She felt positively weak and her head was still muzzy. Peering at herself in the mirror, she looked frightful. Baggy eyed from the crying, stale mascara on her cheeks. 'Come on girl, you can do this,' She stood under the shower and allowed the warmth to surround her.

Dee's parents were in the kitchen frying breakfast. She declined to eat much other than a fried egg on toast. She felt a little queasy. The plan was that her parents would take her back to the cottage after breakfast.

Tom was waiting at the door. He had run her a bath having been pre warned she had been sick again. He held her around the waist and led her upstairs. He gently helped her in the bath and he would have stayed with her, but she wanted him to see to her parents.

As Dee lay in the bath, the door creaked open a little and in walked Mog. It made Dee chuckle. She leant over the side and stroked him. He had obviously missed her and picked up that something was wrong. At the same time, she was not sure if it were her imagination, but sun seemed to glisten through the opaque window and made the water shimmer a little. She often felt a little uneasy in the bathroom but today she felt comfortable and enjoyed the soak for longer than normal.

It was eleven thirty when her parents took their leave. She couldn't put it off any longer, she needed to ring Mel.

Chapter 32

'Dee, oh Dee; I can't believe this is happening.' A sobbing Mel answered the phone.

'I know Mel, I know.'

'I can't believe he would do that to us, to the children. I wouldn't have stopped him seeing them.'

'He was obviously in a bad place. I just wish I had heard my phone earlier, then we could have got there in time and this wouldn't have happened...'

'Dee, don't try to blame yourself for that. The blame is all mine, isn't it? I was the one who left him, I wish now I had just given him notice at least. I was just scared he would stop me.'

'Look Mel, you did what you had to do for yourself and the kids. Geoff had a choice. He could have learned to live with it and so I don't know why he chose this path?'

'The police won't release him yet, pending

investigation and possibly a post - mortem.'

'Do the kids know?'

No, not yet. I need to get my head round it first.'

'Yeah, me and Tom are struggling with finding him.'

'I know Dee, it was mean of him to do that to you.'

'He didn't have anyone else though, did he? Who else could have found him?' there was hint of malice in Dee's voice and Mel had noticed it but chose not to respond.

She said, 'I have got to message his workplace. I am just going to ask Mark to do it. I can't face anyone asking questions. I am dreading the cremation. All his work cronies looking at me and wondering why he did it. Perhaps they will feel sorry for me and not judge me, they probably won't know I left him; will they?'

'Don't worry Mel, I'm sure they will be sympathetic. I must go now; I am feeling sick again. Ring me and let me know when you will be coming.'

Tom hugged her tightly.

Dee snuggled up to him and said, 'Every time I close my eyes; I see the person without the face. When I sleep, I see it too and the tree. I'm sorry Tom I have never even asked you how you are. I am so selfish.'

'I'm alright, just worried about you and you're not selfish.'

'What time are we going to the park with Abbie?' Dee

tried to distract herself with positive things.

'We have to meet there at three so plenty of time to relax. Shall we look at some flooring online now and see which one will work?'

'Yeah, just let me have a bit of a rest.'

Tom watched as she slid back under the duvet and lay staring at the ceiling. Her eyes felt ever so heavy again and the pain above her temple started again. She shut her eyes and fell asleep and shortly afterward started to dream.

A woman was sitting in the cottage garden with a basket of flowers. She smiled at Dee and beckoned her to sit down next to her. It was Tom's mum. Dee sat next to her, and Tom's mum smiled and squeezed her hand, warm from the baking sun. They laughed together and then Dee was awake once more. She woke feeling exhilarated. She wanted to be back in the dream, feeling happy and at peace. She relayed the story to Tom.

'My mother was always there for when people needed her, they all used her for that and yet when she needed them to be there; they stayed away. No one understood alcoholism. Friends she had had for years shunned her and her own sister just told her to pull herself together. I often feel guilty I wasn't around for her enough. I was always working but I should have made time. That is why she spent so much time in the garden. She felt the fresh air did her some good.'

Chapter 33

It was a windy but bright afternoon. Abbie came rushing over to greet them. She leapt at Tom wanting to be swung around, which he did obligingly. She looked at Dee and asked to be passed over for a cuddle. Dee held her very tightly and stroked her hair.

'Right, do you want to go on the swing or slide first? Come on I'll race you,' Dee placed the little girl on the ground and off they sprinted.

There was a lot of laughter, they made a happy group. Julia and Patrick and the twins and Dee, Tom and Abbie. When Abbie's foster parent arrived she started to cry again.

'Will I be able to live with you Dee? Will you be my new mummy?' Abbie desperately jumped on Dee's knee as if somehow Dee could stop her being taken. Dee held her tightly and started to cry herself.

'I want you to live with us Abbie, we'll try and see but we can't promise.' Tom led Abbie to the door helping her put her coat on and cheerfully said they would see her next week.

Dee tried to put a brave face on, but the tears continued. Julia tried to comfort her which made her cry more.

'Come on Dee, I'm sure one day this will happen for you. Just stay positive,'

'Okay Julia, we'll get back home now. Dee needs more rest after what she's been through and everything...'

'At least I have got the week off work.' Dee got up to go.

'Well then why don't I pop round to you for coffee about eleven tomorrow? Julia said hopefully.

Back at the cottage she started to busy herself making a mood board and listing things she would do that week while she was off work. She would order the furniture for Abbie's room and arrange to go shopping with her mum for the bedding and accessories. Of course, she would need toys and computer desk and clothes. There was so much to do. Tom listened to her plans. He had to tell her that the right thing was to hold off as there was nothing concrete yet. They may not get Abbie. Her heart felt heavy again, but when Tom saw that her face fell he smiled and told her to go ahead. She felt warm when she realized how much she mattered to him.

Chapter 34

On Sunday night Claire was sitting at home reflecting on what Dee had gone through. Claire, being Claire, knew it would be a long time before Dee got over this. She expected she would need months off work. She knew her friend and she had extraordinarily little resilience.

Claire herself was more contented than ever though. She was deep into planning her trip to Syria on the first of September. Karis had just moved in with her and they were getting on well. Karis had started an online health and social care course and when they returned from Syria, she had ambitions to start her nurse training. She adored Claire and saw her as a role model. They nurtured one another and as a result they both stopped self- harming. They talked things through with one another now instead. They had shared their histories and knew each other's secrets. It was the mother-daughter relationship they had both so desperately wanted in their lives.

Claire's mum had virtually given up playing for the sympathy vote and just messaged infrequently and Karis's mum, although jealous of Claire, saw Karis weekly for coffee. Deep down she could see the positive influence Claire was having on her once lost daughter. She would never admit it though.

It was a late night at Mel's new home. She sat staring into space, chastising herself for being a bad person, for driving Geoff to take his own life. How could she ever be happy now? The kids would never forgive her as they grew up and understood why he had done it. She was doomed. Mark sat with her listening to her woe. He brought in the philosophical side and reassured her she was a good person. He thought a lot of Mel and hoped in time they may grow close. He said that this news would need incredibly careful handling. He was a vicar of a new parish, with a housekeeper who had left her abusive husband and her husband had now killed himself. It was not the usual introduction to a new community.

Chapter 35

For the first time since Geoff died, Dee slept okay. No faces in the night. When she awoke the next morning, Tom had already left for work. He had left a note to say, 'phone me if you need to and I will come home.'

Dee looked out at the hazy sunny day. A little chilly but bright. She looked at the daffodils edging the path and decided she would go out and cut some. She would make the most of this time off work.

Dressed in a chunky blue jumper she took a basket out the cupboard and cut a few daffs. She did enough for Julia and her mum as well. She felt cheery and content in the quiet of the garden and started to do some weeding. At eleven the doorbell rang, and Julia and the twins were at the door. She had baked some scones that they now ate hot, with jam and cream and Julia remarked how good they were. She had put the coffee machine on, and the aroma filled the house. Only Mog was dissatisfied that his quiet had been shattered by the twins running around.

It was strange Dee thought, but the cottage started to feel more homely to her. She started to believe it was her home. She showed an impressed Julia the plans for the bedroom furniture and the mood board for the kitchen.

'How are you feeling now after the shock last week Dee?' Julia asked empathetically.

'I guess I'm trying not to think about it and to try to focus on positive things. I do feel still I should have tried to get Mel to handle things differently, but Tom keeps reminding me that I did but she would not listen. It's just sad that the kids will grow up without their dad now though.'

'It's no- one's fault. The best of people can take their lives. It happens...'

The rest of the day sailed by. She had now familiarized herself with the kitchen and where things were. She and Tom had come up with a shared housework routine. They were a team. It was never going to be a big romance for either of them, but it was comfortable. They rarely argued and if they did it was short-lived with one of them usually breaking the ice and saying they were sorry. They did not sulk, shout or swear. Dee had always experienced that in other relationships. There was even half an hour left over for Dee to read a magazine before Tom arrived back.

As he opened the door, the smell of beef casserole hit him. It made him feel warm inside. He breathed in and grinned.

'It reminds me of my childhood. Before Dad passed, Mum was a contented woman. There were always fresh flowers, clean linen on the beds and a house full of friends and family.' Tears glinted in his eyes and Dee realized he was remembering her demise into alcoholism.

'You see, when dad died, she wanted to escape to a simpler life in the country away from London and the social scene. She just didn't feel a part of it anymore. That's why we left our big house and settled for a three bedroomed cottage.'

Tom hugged Dee and they shared a tender kiss.

'Thanks for phoning me at lunch. I've had a better day today. It was good to spend time in the garden and have Julia round. I'm beginning to feel more at home here.'

'Good, I am glad you are feeling less upset.'

'Yeah, and I haven't missed work at all. I have done some gardening and ordered the furniture for the bedroom.'

'And still made time to make yourself look gorgeous.' Tom chuckled admiring her long, tousled red locks.

'Tom, did you really mean it when you said it would be okay for me to give up work, because I have been thinking about whether I would miss it and I don't think I would.'

'I would love you to give up work and focus on family life and runnning the home. Then at weekends we can just socialize and go on day trips I have told you don't worry about the money.' He looked at her earnestly.

'Well, I was discussing it with mum and she said she would retire if I stopped working. Well, Kate will be around after August when she has had the baby and Julia next door. What if you get bored of me next year though and I haven't got a job?' Dee looked down at the floor and remembered the past rejections she had had from men.

'I've told you that won't happen Dee, how could I get bored of you?' he picked her up and carried her upstairs. 'The casserole won't burn.'

Each day that week she did different things. She met with her mum, Claire and Julia and had a night at the pub with Tom. The furniture had been delivered and between them they organised the bedroom. It looked stunning, a proper little girl's room. It was just sad that they could not show it to Abbie as they couldn't get her hopes up, it wouldn't be fair.

Dee spoke to Mel daily on the phone. The conversation was circular. Mel was criticising herself for leaving and Dee trying to reassure her that she did what she thought was best; even though deep-down Dee didn't believe this. Dee had felt all along that Mel should have just moved locally and that way Geoff could have seen the kids regularly. Who knows maybe they could have reconciled after Geoff had received help. Mel would sometimes cry on the phone, sometimes get angry with Geoff, sometimes feel sorry for herself and worry what people thought of her. Mel's own parents had been shocked and angry at her for leaving. Mel would be coming back on Monday to see the funeral director now that the body had been released, the police satisfied he had taken his own life.

Dee decided she would stay on sick leave until after the funeral, which would be another couple of weeks. Her GP had agreed she needed time to get over the shock of finding her friend hanging.

On the way to the self-esteem group, Dee had sounded Claire out on the idea of her resigning to be a homemaker. Claire initially laughed thinking it was some kind of wind up but once she knew Dee was being serious, she bit her tongue and said she was happy at the way her life was turning out and that she could always go back in the future. Once a nurse, always a nurse . Deep down Claire thought it the wrong move, especially if the fostering didn't happen. For Claire, her job was her life and her independence. Even if she won a million on the lottery she would be involved in nursing.

Self-esteem session eight was about reviewing and adapting core beliefs about yourself.

Looking for evidence that challenges your views of yourself. Are you dismissing the evidence to say that you are good enough, likeable, not stupid, attractive and so forth. What evidence is there to say that your core beliefs are either right or wrong. Most of the time it is just a feeling rather than a fact.

Then the idea is to write down what your new core beliefs are and keep reading them through.

Could Dee now think she was likeable and good enough? She had made new friends, had a new partner and a new life ahead of her. Did she now feel good enough about herself and likeable? Yes, she was beginning to think she was okay and that the right kind of people could like her.

As a nurse manager, the nature of the job meant that people were bound not to like you sometimes as you are asking them to do things they don't want to do. The job was partly about having to pull people up on not doing things right. That would never make you popular.

Even her weight didn't seem to bother her so much now, Tom found her attractive, and Kate would often comment on her hair or dress sense. That was it, even Kate liked her. Kate who was glamorous and popular and about to become a yummy mummy. Kate had even just purchased a four by four; white of course.

Dee wrote down her new core belief. 'I do like myself and sometimes I am not liked by others but that doesn't mean I am not likeable.'

'I am good enough and am doing lots of new things, such as making a new home and a network for myself. I can feel I belong in my new village.'

Claire had reflected that she too was beginning to feel good enough. Karis thought so and the Red Cross were eager to employ her, despite all the competition. Regarding her mum, she had seen so many different sides to her. She had seen her go into a victim mode, the remorseful mode and then revert to her stand-offish mode. She had decided that actually it wasn't that she wasn't good enough, it was her mum who wasn't good enough for her.

As the two friends drove home, they reflected on what

a difference the group had made to them both and they considered the new opportunities that life had presented. They both still needed to keep reminding themselves what they had learned, but in a short space of time, both friends had begun to view themselves differently and change their lives. Changing yourself can be frightening they reflected. Some people do not want you to change either. How can others continue treating you badly if you stand up for yourself, if you have more friends or more social confidence? No, some people want you to stay passive and grey, to blur into the background. Who else can they use as a physical or emotional punchbag if you change?

'It's a pity Mel didn't do the group, maybe she would have been able to stand up to Geoff and demand he stopped drinking and …' an irritated Claire interrupted Dee.

'And she may have just got another back hander. It's a real shame though that Geoff ended up feeling so hopeless that this was his only option, especially when there are so many helplines like the Samaritans.'

Dee thought for a moment and answered, 'I guess suicide is the ultimate self-harm isn't it.'

They changed the subject to Syria and the preparations. They discussed Karis's progress with her course and how Dee was getting on with the cottage refurb.

When the weekend came it was Tom and Dee's turn to entertain Kate and Ben for Saturday lunch. Tom had done his flagship meal which was chicken curry and Dee had made a homemade lemon meringue pie. They had been in the kitchen together preparing the food and had Spanish guitar music playing. Dee was thinking how relaxing it was and how it felt like they were a unit. They had Mog and now just needed a child then they would be a proper family.

Kate was now twenty-six weeks pregnant and still tiny to look at, but she reported feeling more tired. In fact, she had given up work on a whim. As a temp you only needed to give one week's notice. She was excited to hear that Dee too had given in her notice and would finish work by mid-June. They discussed what they would do together over the summer and how Dee would be able to help her when the baby was born at the beginning of August.

'Can you imagine how nice the summer will be Dee, then if you get Abbie, imagine what Christmas will be like?' Kate beamed over the dinner table to Dee and Tom.

'If we get Abbie, it's a big "if" at the moment,' Dee said in a despondent tone of voice.

'Why wouldn't you? You are in a stable relationship, financially secure with a great house. I thought they were desperate for foster parents anyway?' Ben responded in an upbeat manner.

'I think we are just worried because obviously the

relationship is still new and we're not married or anything yet,' Tom jumped in to support Dee.

'That was a point,' Dee thought. 'The word marriage had never been discussed. Did Tom want to marry her?'

'I don't think being married or not will make a difference these days, any way can't single people foster? So just because there are two of you,' Kate acted as cheer-leader.

'We'll see, Julia has put a character reference forward so that was kind of her,' Dee tried to rally round.

They all went to the local for a drink when the pub opened at six. Most of the villagers seemed to know her name and greet her warmly. She thought it was possibly because they were eager to see Tom happy after losing his mum so tragically.

Chapter 36

At Mel's home there had been some welcome events that surprised her. The new congregation and church stalwarts had rallied round her. Mark had obviously done a good job of telling them that she had escaped an abusive marriage and he had rescued her and given her a respectable job. How unfortunate it now was that Geoff had taken his life and the children were now fatherless. What a martyr Mel had been for such a long time, but then he added that it was sad and that Geoff couldn't have been in his right mind.

Mel had been inundated with visitors offering help with childcare or a shoulder to cry on. She had dreaded being a burden to their new vicar, but it was quite the opposite. They thought both their new vicar and his housekeeper were wonderful. If she could just get through the guilt and the practicalities of the funeral and selling the house, then she could really start her new life.

She had tentatively started to think she did deserve to be happy and maybe, just maybe, this could be with Mark. He looked at her a certain way sometimes and was very loving towards the kids. When he hugged her recently, she felt he had held onto her longer. So many times, she had had to stop herself from reaching for his lips. She dreaded the funeral though, surely Geoff's social work cronies would know that she had left him. She had taken a courtesy call from his manager asking if there was any support she needed and suspected cards had been delivered to the house that she wouldn't have received yet. Perhaps they thought she had gone to stay with relatives for a bit.

Monday came and Mel and Mark met with the funeral director. Mel had been offered the opportunity to see Geoff's body, but she declined. She became overcome with angst and felt faint, she needed Mark there to bolster her. She had chosen a cremation as that was what they had talked about and decided on a non -religious service as he was not a believer. Who was going to talk about Geoff at the service? He had no family. She would ask his social work manager to do the honour.

After the visit to the funeral director, they met Dee for coffee at their usual haunt. When the two friends met, they clasped each other firmly both moved by recent events. Mark decided to go shopping for an hour to give them time alone. Mel told Dee about all the support she had had since moving, except from her own parents who had been critical of her sneakiness and deception, not just toward Geoff but them as well.

'Dee, have you recovered from finding Geoff? Are you still having flashbacks and nightmares?'

'No nightmares, but the odd vision.' Dee reflected.

'That's a relief. I've been having nightmares, it's always the same thing. I am standing there alone, and people are laughing at me and walking away from me.' Mel looked sadly at the floor.

'You had those dreams when you were young as well,' Dee reminisced.

'Yeah, I guess it's all about been judged badly and rejected; because of what I've done. Geoff's killed himself because of me. I should have done things differently. I've been selfish Dee, haven't I?", Mel looked searchingly into Dee's eyes.

'You weren't to know he would do this as you would have done things differently. It is one of those things Mel. When are you going to tell the kids?'

'After the funeral. It is weird that I'm less worried about talking to them about it now than discussing it with them when they're older, when they will want to know the full details. What will I say? Well I got so fed up, so I ran away and left your dad a note and a hotpot and oh by the way I moved two hundred miles away to live with a vicar. Can you imagine it?'

'They will understand that you were frightened of their father and you hoped he would still have regular contact with them.' Dee looked her squarely in the eyes.

'The funeral's next Tuesday. Will you come Dee?'

'Of-course I will come. I will always be there for you, Mel.'

‘In a couple of months will you and Tom come for a weekend. Mark is eager to get to know you and Tom. The weather will be warmer, and we can take the kids to the beach and everything.’

‘I’d like that.’

After the catch up, Dee drove to see her own parents. Dee’s mum had nipped to the shop, but her dad came in from his workshop and hugged his daughter.

‘We never get time to speak on our own Dad, how are you? You look tired.’

‘You know a few aches and pains, a bit more tired but I am nearly sixty. Come on let us get the kettle on. How are you?’

'I'm sleeping alright and just keeping myself busy. Thanks again for the dressing table you made, it looks beautiful in what we hope will be Abbie's bedroom.'

‘Hi love, just nipped out to get some cream cakes in case you popped in after seeing Mel, how is she? Dee’s mum stumbled through the door laden with shopping bags.

Dee filled them in with Mel's situation and then they switched to plans of the kitchen work.

When Dee left, Roy turned to Shirley and said, ‘She noticed I am looking tired.’

Shirley grabbed his hand and they both started to cry.

Dee got home and rustled up a chicken salad for tea. She wished she lived closer to her parents. She thought about how pale her dad looked earlier. She could never imagine life without them and wondered how Tom had managed to cope being without his. She walked upstairs to the new child's bedroom and admired it. Tom had done a good job of sanding the floor and varnishing it. The dressing table her dad had made took pride of place. It was just like the one Dee used to have and there was a hairbrush and mirror set as a centerpiece, that her mum had bought.

Soft sunlight shone through the window. She was drawn to look out into the garden. They needed to get a swing for when Abbie came. She fantasized about a child or children running around the garden, bringing it to life. It deserved that.

'Hi,' Tom shouted up the stairs. She walked down, feeling ever so slightly lucky at how her life had turned out. She still had the nagging feeling though that something was going to go wrong....

As the week past, Dee started to dread the idea of going back to work. Her heart would start to beat faster, and she would get a tension headache when she thought of it.

'Don't go back then,' it was simple for Tom.

Less simple for Dee. She did not want to let Claire

down and feared what people would think. It was tempting though.

That night she attended the last self-esteem group

'Now a recap on what you all need to keep doing,' Joy enthused.

'Number 1- Remember to keep making your rules for living more flexible so that they are easier to achieve. Think before you attack, or aim to people please, or before you avoid or be passive - what am I achieving? Is it making the situation worse? Is it making me feel worse?'

'Number 2- Remember to keep challenging your negative core beliefs about yourselves or others. Is there contradictory evidence to show that what I am thinking isn't true? Am I dismissing positives about myself, the world around me and other people? Can I be less harsh on myself and others and less critical of myself and others?'

'Number 3- Remember not to predict that bad things might happen- as this is when you go into avoidance, or people pleasing. Just see what happens and deal with it if it does. Remember all the bad things you have had to deal with in your life and have come through the other end. Even if the bad thing does happen, you will cope.'

Claire and Dee reflected on how they thought the group had helped them. They thanked Joy. Little did they know that the reason Joy did the group was because she sometimes slipped into low self esteem and needed to also use the strategies. Joy, however, was a firm believer that everyone struggled with self -esteem it was just a matter of to what extent.

On the way back Dee filled Claire in on her life. Claire, on the other hand, had little to report. For once her life seemed without drama and she had a clear pathway ahead. Claire, unlike Dee, did not worry about the if's, buts and maybes. She knew worrying was futile.

On the Thursday, Dee and her mum went shopping for the bedding and curtains.

Over lunch, Dee said, 'Mum, I thought dad looked a little tired the other day. Has he been overdoing things again?'

'You know your dad, he never stops, and he forgets he's getting older,' her mum hid behind the menu as she spoke.

'I think I'll have a tuna salad love, what are you having?' her mum then quickly changed the conversation.

'Yes, I'll join you. I have lost a little weight lately, but I am still more than fourteen stone. Tom likes big portions and I end up eating the same. I need to be stricter,' Dee said eyeing up the dessert menu.

Over dinner that night Tom asked Dee if she would go away for a week with him at the end of June. He had planned a surprise break not far from Mel's, so they could go for a weekend with her first and then travel on to their location. He wouldn't say where they were going but he asked her to make sure she packed her new cocktail dress.

The following week on a bright sunny morning Geoff was cremated. Jan the social work manager said a few words about how he inspired the trainees, how he fought to get the services his clients needed and how much he would be missed. The lay preacher said kind words about his past and personality. There at the front stood Mel, flanked by her parents on one side and Mark on the other.

From a few rows behind, Dee could study the back of Mel's neck; she could hear her crying. Dee cried too and Tom held her hand tightly. It seemed like forever before the curtains closed and the organic wicker basket coffin was gone.

The children were not in attendance but back at the house being looked after by a trusted church warden.

There was a small wake. When Dee and Tom sat with Mel and Mark the conversation was about day-to-day stuff. It was as if Mel were relieved it was over. She had even started clearing the house of valuables and had instructed a house clearance firm about the rest, it could be auctioned then. She would make a tidy sum, but of course the life insurance would not pay out, not for suicide.

Tom and Mark went to the bar together as Tom wanted to discuss their plans for their visit in June. Dee had never felt uncomfortable with Mel before, but now she felt strained. She wasn't sure what to say.

'It doesn't feel real still,' Mel searched her friend's eyes.

'No. I guess it won't for a while. How are you coping, not just with the loss but all the paperwork and bits?'

'Well, if it weren't for Mark I wouldn't be. My parents don't want to know. They don't say it directly but the way they look at me is awful. I miss seeing you as well.'

'It will get easier when the house is sorted. Have you not thought about coming back now though, no need to escape?'

'Only to escape my guilt I suppose. I want to give what I am doing a go, Dee. So far, I like it. It is a big house, a huge garden for the kids to play in and not far to the beach. I think the change will do me good. I could never think about living back at the house again. There would be too many bad memories.'

'How are the kids?'

'Josh asked after his dad the other day, so I told him dad had died in an accident when he fell off a tree. At least that's partly right…'Josh cried and said he will see him again in heaven so now every night we say a prayer for him. He made him a card as well and left it on the TV, so he can see it from his home in the clouds. It broke my heart when I saw it there. I feel so ashamed of myself. Abandoning him when he needed me, after he helped me so much over the years. It just got too tiring and too upsetting…'

The men returned with soft drinks and with Mel's parents in tow. So Dee and Tom excused themselves to let them have time alone.

'How are you doing?' Tom whispered into Dee's ear.

'I would like to go as soon as we can, I feel shattered. It would look bad if we left too soon though. Can we go outside for a bit?'

Dee grabbed hold of Tom's hand and led him into the pub garden. They sat on a bench in a quiet area. She looked round at the weathered wooden tables, and the long grass growing around the bins. She always thought pubs were strange places for wakes, the somber mourners having to mingle with excited children running around and adults out on a jolly.

'I'm sorry Tom, meeting me has brought a lot of drama. You had a quiet life before me. You only buried your mum last year, is this bringing memories up for you?'

'A bit yeah, when my mum died it was all a blur. The saddest thing was all the friends that had stayed away because of her drinking all showed up on the day. Gave me their condolences and I just wanted to tell them all to piss off, as they had not been there for her through her bad times. Funerals are often a farce, aren't they?'

'I know. It's just a shame the person never gets to hear what nice things people say about them isn't it?'

An awkward hour later they left.

Chapter 37

Dee's thoughts kept focusing on the visit of the fostering agency worker Yvette the following Friday. She feared that Yvette may interrogate her about her mental health following the suicide. Somehow, she suspected that all the social workers would know about Geoff dying and Dee finding him hanging. Irrational she knew but she couldn't' shake the thought.

The nightmares had returned, Dee's sleep was all over the place and as a result so was Tom's. She had felt anxious again about being left alone in the house and had spent more time at her parents and Julia's. She had seen the GP again, who signed her off until the end of May. He had wanted her to consider anti-depressants, but she had declined due to fear it would affect their fostering application. She had also declined counselling.

On the Friday morning the doorbell rang promptly at nine thirty and there stood a casually dressed Yvette, from the fostering agency. 'Hi, what a beautiful looking home, her eyes sparkled as she stepped through the door. Dee thought that, just like Joy from the group, Yvette's out-fit was so together. This time her blond hair was cut into a neat bob and she wore a pale blue flowery shirt with navy chinos.

'Hi, come in. We've just made a fresh pot of coffee, can I get you one?' Tom ushered her into the sitting room. Yvette was greeted by Mog and by the sun shining towards the hearth. Dee sat down awkwardly, wishing she had offered to make the drinks; she was beginning to shake.

Dee offered Yvette the armchair by the fireplace. She then started to worry that the throw on it may have smelt a little of Mog and what would Yvette make of that? Would she write it in her notes?

'Now I know you are probably nervous, but the purpose of this first meeting is really for us to all get to know one another and to discuss the application journey and both our and your own expectations. Can we start by talking about the reasons you have for wanting to foster?'

Tom did nearly all the talking. Dee felt too worried about saying the wrong thing. She tried to nod and smile in the right place and to look enthusiastic. Really, she wanted to run out the room. She felt ridiculous, she was a ward manager and yet she was somehow frightened of being judged inadequate. She pictured Joy sitting next to her wishing her well and this gave her a boost. Then she started to feel like talking.

A couple of hours later, they were all looking around the house together and discussing gardening tips. Yvette of course wasn't there to trip them up, not to judge but to empower people like Tom and Dee to be successful. She had so many kids needing a placement.

They would meet again in May, to do a more detailed suitability check and then they would attend the course in June and decisions would be made by the end of August if all was well.

Chapter 38

The weeks following the death of Geoff, saw Mel vary from being a nervous wreck; feigning illness and staying in bed to cheerfully going about daily business as if it had never happened. Mark never quite knew what mood she would be in that day. He was frequently having to cancel his own commitments to caretake the kids, but the congregation were rallying around.

Mel was doing housekeeping chores, but housework had never been her forte however she was good at rustling up a hearty meal. They would all sit together at night and eat. Like a normal family, they would sit and play with the kids, read them a story before bed and at weekends would go for a walk on the beach, after the Sunday service of course. Both tried to fight their growing attachment because it seemed immoral and inappropriate but it was futile. The congregation could see it as well, but rather than viewing it as sordid they found it endearing. Their wonderful bright young vicar was rescuing a woman who had been a victim and not only that he was prepared to take the children on as well.

Mel had considered maybe she had ended up been rescued again; just like Geoff had done for her before. How ironic, though, that Geoff had not been able to rescue himself.

Chapter 39

At her next GP appointment at the end of May, Dee was happy to report that she was too nervous to return to work, ever. Human resources were irritated with her as she refused to work her notice. She was actively breaking her contract they said, but Dee stuck to her guns and Nurse Dee was no longer.

Claire would normally be livid, but she had mellowed. Dee wasn't surprised, she had seen the more empathic Claire.

Yvette visited again with a questionnaire. This time the question of health came up and they had to sign to give permission for the GP to complete a medical questionnaire. So, Dee poured out how difficult it had been finding Geoff, but how now the nightmares were infrequent. Yvette was sympathetic and pleased things were improving.

They talked more about how they wanted to foster Abbie and Yvette disclosed she already knew from information Julia had provided. She said what a good egg Julia was. They told her how their relationship with Abbie had steadily grown and their fondness for her and what they could offer her. They had been meeting with her most Sundays and taking time to get to know what she liked to play with, what stories she liked, how she liked her hair and all the other things they had picked up on. They had kept a note of them all.

Dee was relieved that Yvette was beaming when she left. She even gave Dee a reassuring pat on the shoulder and waved as she drove off which they considered to be positive.

Dee's parents came around and they ate a ploughman's lunch.

The builder had knocked the kitchen through to the dining room and Dee's dad had been coming most days to plaster and lay flooring and he was just about ready to paint. Sometimes Dee's mum would come too and join Dee in gardening or visiting; but shopping was their favourite pastime.

Dee would notice how tired and grey her dad looked some days and yet he would only have a short break for a drink. He never seemed hungry.

'I wish my parents lived in the village.' Dee sighed after she had waved them off that night.

'Yeah, that would be great. I will see if I can put the feelers out to see if anyone is looking to move. Do you think they would consider it?' Tom reflected.

'It'll be too expensive for them Tom.'

'Do you think they would rent? The cottage by the church is a rental you know. People don't tend to stay that long. It's a bit pricey for the size. I'll speak to Mr Banks; he owns it and see if he thinks it will come up again in the next year. If they sell theirs, well maybe they could use the money to pay the rent. Or even rent theirs out and use that money toward the rent, maybe we can help as well.'

'Oh my God Tom, can you imagine how fantastic that would be?'

'Yeah, I will get fatter from your mum's cakes. As long as we have our time as well though Dee.'

'You still haven't told me where we are going in a couple of weeks. I don't know what to pack?'

'I've told you, casual for a break by the coast so bring some walking shoes. Whatever you do don't forget that dress.'

'What are you up to Tom? Why won't you just tell me where we are going?'

'Nope, do you fancy a game of cards?' he headed for the sideboard and laughed to himself.

Shirley and Roy were driving home feeling contented that their only child had found the happiness in life that had been such a long time coming.

'When are you going to tell her Roy?' Shirley gave her husband a sideways glance.

'Shirley, I've already told you to drop it. Let them get this fostering process sorted first, you don't want her worrying about anything else, do you?'

'No, but I don't like us keeping things from her. She is always saying how tired you look. I feel bad keeping it from her. She'll be upset that we haven't told her.'

'Do you fancy going to the garden centre tomorrow?' Roy said turning the radio up.

Chapter 40

Mel had been calling Dee less often, maybe twice a week. She was beginning to focus more on the future. The house was due to be auctioned off in the July. Dee had tried to persuade her to come back and live there, or if not live locally, but Mel was keen to continue her new life with Mark. She was hoping that he could be her new partner. She had no intention of returning. The air was so much cleaner by the sea as well.

Dee and Tom were now invited to Kate and Ben's regularly for Saturday night meals. Kate was getting bigger and hated it. She was now thirty- two weeks pregnant. She ached all over and suffered terrible indigestion. Her hair was dry and brittle and her skin itchy. She frequently felt irritable and so was always glad to see Dee. When she spent the evening in a foursome she couldn't argue with Ben. He'd become the one that she took her stress out on.

Kate and Ben's extension had been completed and the home looked like something out of a glossy magazine, but it had not made Kate happy. She was beginning to think nothing would. She had passed the thrill of being pregnant and just wanted the baby out now.

'Hi Kate, you look well. How are you doing?' Dee held a hand-tied bundle of roses fresh from the cottage garden. She looked at Kate and knew there was something not right.

The men had already drifted out into the garden, beers in hand. 'Now the weather's getting better we must try for that barbie soon,' Ben looked over for approval from Kate, but as usual she ignored him and ushered Dee into the kitchen.

'We've just cooked pasta, hope that's okay?' she half-heartedly began to toss the salad ready to serve.

'Kate, is everything alright?'

'I'm not sleeping well; the baby is laying awkwardly, and I hate feeling so big. I detest the way I look and dare not say that to anyone as they think I'm being ungrateful and somehow precious, I guess.'

'I get it Kate, but it won't be for too much longer, I hope. Are you worrying about things?'

'Well, me and Ben we're only just a new item, but it feels like we're an old married couple. Life feels a bit much the same. At first, it felt great. It's just…'

'Is grub up then Kate?' Ben burst into the conversation.

As usual the night consisted of catching up about the situation with the fostering process, Tom and Dee's household improvements and Kate's experiences with midwives. Dee tried to engineer to wash-up beside Kate so they could have a further chat, but Ben told them to leave the pots he would do them later. Dee whispered to Kate that she would phone her when she knew Ben would be at work and they said their goodbyes.

On the way home Dee filled Tom in on what Kate had told her.

'Oh no, what did you make of it? Do you think she's only tired and grumpy or do you think they're in trouble?' Tom frowned.

'I don't know I'll give her a ring. Hopefully, she will feel differently when the baby comes. There's nothing worse than not sleeping. Kate's so tiny that if baby's pressing on her it must be uncomfortable poor thing. I probably won't notice if I get pregnant being big already.'

'You aren't big, you're just right. Stop putting yourself down.' Tom pinched her leg.

Dee was starting to feel nervous as the course was the next day. It was an introduction to fostering and what support people would get, common issues that children would experience when they start living in a foster placement and so forth.

Dee was thinking about her old job. She wondered how Sophie the junior nurse was and felt bad that she hadn't been able to do anything to help her. She had asked Claire to try to nurture her, but Sophie had again been avoidant. Sophie, instead, was putting all her energy into trying to 'people please' with Sam, to get into her good books. She hoped that it would make Sam nicer to her. Although she tried hard, Sam still was only superficially nice and then bitched about her to the health care support workers and made fun of her. Sam wasn't always sensitive, often doing it in front of Sophie's face. Sophie had now gone on the sick again apparently, saying she was struggling with migraines when really; she was struggling with being bullied and being made to feel she didn't fit in.

Claire had been determined not to leave the situation and decided to call around to see Sophie on spec on the Sunday. Totally irregular practice to try to deal with things out of work, but hey Claire didn't give a damn. She was leaving at the end of August.

'Sophie, I know you are being bullied. Why don't you let human resources know and raise a complaint?' Claire said as she was let into Sophie's flat.

'You know it will make it worse. I am just going to look for another job. I can't be bothered with HR.'

'The thing is Sophie, well, Sam will just keep doing it. It has happened before, but no one would come forward. We need to take her on. I'll help you, between me and you, I'll help you before I go.'

'Thanks Claire, but I have got another interview next week at the private hospital. I've made my mind up.'

Claire walked away feeling despondent. She herself had been bullied and made to feel left out as a child and she hated to think Sam had won. The only thing she could do was to warn her replacement to look out for Sam. No wait she did have another way...Monday morning and Claire rang through to the ward and asked Sam to meet her at lunchtime.

'Hi Sam, thanks for coming do you fancy a coffee?
'

'Ok thanks, what's this about Claire?'

'Well, I need you to move you to another ward due to shortages. I need to move you to ward 40.'

'Surgical. No sorry it's not my thing. Can you get someone else?'

'No, I need someone with experience Sam. You will need to start next week. If I can recruit someone soon, I'll move you back.'

'I'll speak to the union; I don't want to move.'

'You know I wouldn't ask unless the service required it. We have to meet the needs of the service and you know that it's in your contract that we can move you. I'm sure you'll get used to it.'

Sam stomped out the office and Claire chuckled. The ward manger on surgical hated Sam. She would make her life miserable and hopefully Sam would leave; not before being put down and made to feel how she had made Sophie feel. Claire phoned Sophie and told her the news, and asked if she would come back, but Sophie had already made her mind up to leave. The private sector was offering more wages and a personal development package.

When Sophie put the phone down, she was smiling. She had already started counselling to increase her self-confidence and was hoping to start her new job afresh, as a new Sophie.

Chapter 41

There were four other couples on the fostering course, one single sex couple called Ian and Jimmy. Dee and Tom sat with them and soon made easy conversation. The first day was all about hopes and dreams as to what fostering could do for them. There was a lot of group-work and Dee found it inspiring to hear each person's story.

At the end of the day Tom was feeling so uplifted that he decided they would call to see Mr Banks to ask about the cottage and when it would be up for rent again. Apparently, it would be occupied until Christmas and then the tenant would be moving out. The rent was expensive, but when they discussed it further at home, Tom decided he could help top it up if Dee's parents wanted it. They were meeting for lunch on the Sunday so they would bring it up then.

'Tom, everything just seems to be falling into place for us at the minute, I know Geoff died, but it feels things with us were just made to be. I know I sound weird, don't I?'

'If we can get Abbie and if your parents live up the lane, you are right things would be perfect. Just like you, I never thought life would change for me either. Come here and let me kiss you.'

'I still can't see what you see in me Tom?'

'I see a caring and hardworking, intelligent family woman and you're everything I want and need. Why what do you see in me? I mean I am muddied up most of the time. I'm overweight and just a steady Eddie.'

'Aren't you forgetting your other qualities, or do I need to remind you?' Dee teased flashing her eyes.

The rest of the week at the fostering course was on a similar theme each day. It was intense at times with lots of information: from first aid to how to handle a tantrum. By the end of Friday Tom and Dee were shattered and knew that all they had to do now was wait for the panel to decide whether they were suitable to foster and whether they could have Abbie. They should know August time.

On the Saturday, Dee met up with Claire who introduced her to Karis. They met at Claire's and filled each other in with their latest news.

'I'd have loved to have seen Sam's face when you told her you were moving her. Good one Claire,' Dee laughed.

'I'll give her two weeks there before she'll up and go. Hopefully not to wherever Sophie will be working.'

'Did you really need anyone on surgical?'

'No, not really,' Claire winked at Dee.

Dee tutted a little but sniggered at the same time. That was what she liked about Claire, she just got things done. Dee wanted to be a person who got things done, without ruminating and being indecisive. Without worrying what people thought of her or dwelling on the consequences. Then she reminded herself she had left work, without giving a thought to what the staff thought of her; all her energy was on home now.

'We're going away for a week on Monday,' Dee announced. 'We are visiting Mel overnight and then going on to wherever. Tom won't tell me anything.'

'That is romantic, hope you're not in a tent. He does like his mud.'

'Doubt it, he told me to pack that cream cocktail dress I bought.'

'The one that you said you would never have the confidence to wear?'

'Yeah, so much for a self -esteem course.'

'I don't know Dee; I think you have got more confident. You would never have had the confidence to jack your job in before or put yourself out there to be scrutinized by social services.'

'True. Look at you as well, off abroad, giving up your important job and giving your mum a piece of your mind.' You have got stronger as well. Well, more emotionally strong, you've always been confident.'

'I guess we should both be glad we did the course in the end then?' Claire smiled wryly remembering the times she wanted to give it up and not bother as she couldn't see the point in it.

Dee had phoned Kate in the week, but she didn't want to talk on the phone suggesting they instead met alone for coffee on the Saturday afternoon. So, after leaving Claire and Karis, feeling upbeat, Dee then dreaded what she suspected was going to be a vastly different scenario with Kate.

They met in a garden centre which had one of those trendy coffee shops inside, that would cheer you up after you had been shopping for growbags and weed-killer.

'Hi Kate,' Dee tried to sound cheerful and hugged her friend.

'Hi, I'll grab the drinks do you want a latte or...'

Once settled down and small talk over Dee ventured.

'What is it, Kate?'

'I don't know really, I guess I am just not sure about me and Ben and now having a baby makes me feel I need to be sure.'

'Tell me more.'

'I think it's just, well I feel like I've lost me a bit. I don't go out to work now or see people much. I don't get to wear nice clothes or go to the gym. I feel like I'm not me anymore and when the baby comes, I'll feel even less like me.'

'You could go back to work couldn't you in the future and go to the gym. You could have a childminder or something.'

'That is the confusing bit, I wanted to be a stay-at-home mum, I wanted to be like you and be content to bake and garden and have the odd pub lunch. Now I don't know what I want, including whether I want Ben.'

'Why don't you just wait and see how you feel when the baby comes. Take it a step at a time. Don't make any drastic decisions now.'

'I don't think I have much choice really.'

'Are you worried about the birth or anything? Is that playing on your mind?'

'Yeah, a little. I don't want any scars or stretchmarks either.'

'Well, I am guessing that most women worry about giving birth and the after-effects on their body,' Dee pondered.

'I guess, but well, we'll see what happens and deal with it then. I am trying not to think too far ahead but it's hard not to.'

'I wish you were feeling happier and settled. I'm sorry you're not,' Dee reflected sadly, trying to look deep into Kate's eyes.

'Do you think you'll try for a baby Dee? After you've got Abbie?'

'I'd like to, but we haven't discussed it yet. We would need to get Abbie settled with us first. I talk about it as if it is going to happen when it probably won't. They probably think we're better suited to another child.'

'How would you feel if you were offered another one?'

'I don't know really; we haven't talked about it. We're just so intent on getting her.'

At the end of the catch -up Dee agreed to phone Kate weekly and do more one- to- one meet ups. Kate needed her.

Sunday lunch was the first meal Dee and Tom had cooked together in their new kitchen diner. They had invested in new kitchen appliances in pastel colours, tea towels to match and new accessories. It was a bright sunny day and with low volume classical music in the background they idly chatted while Tom prepared the main and Dee baked the pudding.

Dee's parents arrived and they all sat down for lunch.

'We've got something to ask you both,' Dee announced. 'You say it, Tom.'

'Well we would love it if you could live nearer to us, especially when we have a family. There is a cottage up the lane, coming up to rent. It will be ready at Christmas We were wondering if…'

'Will you consider living there?' Dee excitedly took over. 'We know you are happy at your own home, but it would be lovely to have you nearer us and Tom and I can help with the rent if you want us to.'

Dee's parents looked at each other and neither knew what to say.

'You are right love, it would be nice to be nearer to you, but we'll have to think it through. It's not ideal moving into a cottage as you're getting older, what with the stairs and often there're small rooms.' Her dad looked concerned.

'Oh, there's a downstairs study that could be made into a bedroom and it has a shower room downstairs as well. You would love the garden. There're fields at the back. We'll walk round in a bit and show you it from the outside.'

'The thing is me and your dad have always lived where we are. It will be hard to move but, like your dad said, you know we would love to be nearer you and we like Julia and Patrick as well, so we'll see.' Shirley looked hopefully at her husband.

'The apple pie is great Dee,' Tom changed the subject not wanting Dee's parents to feel awkward after what he suspected had been a bombshell in the conversation.

After lunch they sauntered around the village, Dee interlinked arms with her dad.

'Well what do you think?' Dee asked after they arrived outside the rented cottage.

'Well, it's bigger than what I thought. Your mum will like it, she's always wanted a cottage in the country.'

'Oh Dee, it's beautiful.' Her mum stood in awe.

'There would be room for a man cave in the garden Mr. Banks said,' Tom threw in as bait.

'Right, well you know I like to do my projects and bits,' Dee's dad started to ponder. Of course, there were many things going on in his mind. He could see there would be several advantages in been closer to Dee.

They all went round to see Julia as they knew that Abbie had arrived there. Julia had done a light tea for all of them. She and Shirley always seemed to find much to talk about, mainly crocheting. Julia was learning it and Shirley was an expert.

Abbie was now fully comfortable in the surroundings. 'Can we go to your house Dee?' Abbie whispered in Dee's ear.

'Not at the moment Abbie, there's stuff all over as we are decorating.'

'Can I live with you soon?' The whole room seemed to go quiet.

'Hey Abbie, look at this. I've got you a new book,' Julia led Abbie into the lounge.

Dee burst out crying and so that Abbie didn't notice she went outside. Tom followed.

'Hey, come here you.' He pulled her into his chest.

'What if we aren't approved Tom? We would have got her hopes up and ours and it would be just terrible.' Dee struggled to catch her breath.

'Look, I can't see any reason why we won't be approved, and I can't see why they wouldn't let us have her. Julia has filled them in on how we are with her. She needs permanent foster care, and she will be next-door-but-one to her brothers. Come on try to think more positively now,' Tom said assertively.

Dee sniffled and blew her nose. 'I will have to tell Abbie I have hay fever.'

They had a lovely afternoon afterwards having walked over to the green and played football. Dee's parents took in the scene and admired the village views.

'Would you want to move here Shirl?' Roy asked his wife.

'I am surprised you don't know the answer already, but I don't know how we will afford to. The rent's going to be so high, and I don't like the idea of either selling or renting out our house. If things go wrong with Dee and Tom, we will all need somewhere to live again.'

'No, we wouldn't sell it. We could rent it out and just hope it doesn't get trashed. The fresh air and country walks might be good for me.' Roy was beginning to see how village life may suit him, but more importantly he knew being closer to Dee would very much suit his wife.

'Can we look at the money situation and see, Roy?'

'Yes, we will do that.' Just then Abbie dragged Roy up to play ball with her. Dee sat next to her mum and reached out for her hand.

‘Mum, do you think you will live here? I’d love it if you could.’

'We'll see love. It's a big step for us.'

Chapter 42

Monday morning came and the drive to Melissa's began. Dee still didn't know where they were going after that. They arrived at the vicarage which was a large Victorian building set in an idyllic position next to the church. Mel's kids greeted them at the door and there was much banter and excitement.

'Mel you look great, you look really healthy,' Dee offered as they escaped into the kitchen to sort out drinks.

'I am feeling good at the mo. It must be the sea air.'

'I've got loads to tell you Mel.'

'We'll have the drinks and you and me will go for a walk without the men for a bit, I'll show you round the town and then we'll come back for lunch. Mark hasn't booked anything in today, so unless someone is dying or dead, we should be alright.'

After coffee, the two friends had a saunter around the small town. Mel told her about her routines and how the kids were and Dee telling her about Abbie and her parents' potential move into the village. They talked continuously and easily. When they stopped to sit in the park Mel turned to Dee. 'Well it's happened, what you didn't think would happen.'

'You mean, you and Mark?'

'Yeah, and Dee, I am so in love and the kids adore him. We'll leave it until early in the New Year and then announce our engagement.'

'I'm really pleased for you but are you sure it's not too soon after Geoff and everything.'

'You want to talk, fostering a child after just meeting Tom,' Mel jibed.

'Yeah, you're right. Let's just hope this time we're both doing the right thing.' They walked arm in arm back to the vicarage, where Tom and Mark were busy making a ploughman's lunch. In the afternoon they had a brisk walk along the beach and again the men took charge of playing with the kids. They had decided to give the best friends time to catch up.

The following day Dee and Tom said their goodbye's and off they went to the mystery location.

'Now Dee before you get too excited, we're only stopping here overnight and then we are off again,' Tom said as they started to head down a long gravel driveway.

A castle appeared through the trees.

Dee said, 'Oh my God Tom, are we staying here?'

'Yep, and we have the place to ourselves tonight. It's all ours.'

'Really, how much was this?'

'Never you mind. At six we will have a private chef arrive to make us our a la carte meal and then it is back to being just me and you. I hope you wear that dress tonight, by the way.'

They spent the day walking around the walled garden, then further round the lake and the wood behind it. They were both in awe of the stone statues and topiary. There was even a walled rose garden, filled with pale pink climbers. The sun beat down as the two walked from bench to bench admiring different perspectives.

Dinner was to be ready for seven thirty so they had chance to spend time in the hot tub together chilling and then had a nap in the four- poster bed.

Dee had time to pamper herself. She tried to remember how to do the smoky eyes and the red lips. She groomed herself like never before, enjoying the luxurious dressing room. Tom was getting ready in the other room so he could be surprised by her makeover. She had tried the cream silky cocktail dress on the week before. She was still snug in it but with a hard intake of breath could do the zip up.

'It's seven Dee, I'm going down see you in a minute,' Tom knocked the door.

She looked at herself in the mirror and yes, she took a selfie (no pout) and felt stupid afterwards, but she wanted to show her mum and dad. As she started down the long flowing grand staircase, she noticed a handsome Tom complete with dinner jacket standing waiting at the bottom of the staircase. His hair newly tousled with gel. He had the biggest smile on his face.

'Stay there, I want to take a photo,' he had his phone prepared and took several shots of Dee posing. Ian the chef then appeared and ushered them to the front of the castle where he took photos of them together.

The meal was superb. Freshly caught salmon was on the menu and after they had finished the dessert, Tom walked over to Dee and got down on one knee and...

'Dee, beautiful, clever, kind Dee will you marry me?'

'I will,' she said shakily. Tom produced a stunning ruby ring.

'To match your gorgeous red hair, Dee.'

Tom said, 'I love you and have loved you since the moment I saw you.' They kissed passionately, and Tom took her by the hand to lead her up the stairs. He picked her up at the bedroom doorway and placed her on the bed. They made love slowly and tenderly.

Dee had a disturbed sleep. She felt a tad uncomfortable in the unfamiliar old room. She listened for creaks and watched to see if the curtains twitched. Tom slept through. The next day they had to leave by eleven. Their next location was a fisherman's cottage overlooking the harbour. They spent the next couple of days meandering around cobbled streets, in and out of antique shops and cafes. At night they strolled around the harbour and beach, finding hillside walks with views and fascinating deserted ruins. Dee and Tom were feeling lucky to be alive.

They were due to head back home on the Saturday, but on the Friday lunch Dee received a text to say that Kate had gone into labour five weeks early and was presently at the maternity department. Knowing that Kate and Ben had no local family, they thought they had better head home in case they were needed.

Chapter 43

Twenty - two hours later baby Jade was delivered. An exhausted Kate practically begged for help. She had an episiotomy and forceps delivery. Kate was traumatised. Although she held her baby and cried and felt exhilarated, she was exhausted and out of it. The midwives had to take little Jade into their care. Kate had to sleep and sleep. The soreness was immense.. Kate had hoped for so much more. She had not quite finished her anti natal class and the birth was supposed to be a wonderful experience.

Tom and Dee were invited to visit on the second day. The maternity team were so concerned that Kate was kept in for monitoring. Jade had slight jaundice.

'Hi, congratulations,' Dee burst through the door.

Ben was holding baby Jade and giving her a bottle, while Kate was propped up on her side looking pale and tired.

'She's gorgeous,' Tom looked longingly at Jade.

'Thanks both,' have a seat where you can. Ben said wearily. He had had little rest, travelling back and forth to the hospital and desperately worrying about Kate.

'Ben, would you mind going with Tom for a coffee so that I can have a girlie chat with Dee?' Kate said.

Ben lay Jade in her cot next to Kate's bed and Kate rolled onto the other side. Ben pretended not to notice and sadly left the room with Tom in tow.

'Come here you, how are you?' Dee grabbed hold of a tearful Kate.

'It was awful Dee, just awful. I'm in so much pain and...'

Dee sat and listened to often a very repetitive account of all aspects of the labour and how she was feeling now.

'I don't think I can cope. She cries a lot, she's always windy and she's awake all night and asleep in the day and...'

'You will manage. It just takes getting used to. Don't forget Ben will be able to do a lot as well, especially if you're bottle feeding.'

'I do want her; I just don't think I'm going to be able to cope with her. I am just hopeless. I can't get her to stop crying and she just seems happier with Ben than me.'

'She's probably picking up on how you are tired and stressed. You'll be fine Kate.'

'Alright you two?' Ben entered the room and an

awkward Tom followed. 'We've bought you a latte each and some chocolate,'

'Is it a skinny latte?' Kate looked only semi interested.

'It doesn't matter Kate you need all your strength at the minute,' Ben said, slightly, irritated, handing Kate the plastic cup.

Dee and Tom promised to keep in touch and left. 'Well, that was a surprise,' Tom said as they left the ward.

'Yeah, she's only tired. When they get home things will be okay. God, we forgot to tell them we are engaged.' Dee laughed. She spent the rest of the day catching up with Claire and Mel and telling them the good news about her engagement.

On the Sunday, Tom arranged for Dee's parents, to come over and meet up with Julia and Patrick, Abbie and the kids. They went out for tea to celebrate.

'Can I be your bridesmaid?' Abbie asked excitedly.

Then Dee's mum announced excitedly that they were interested in the rented house.

'Oh fantastic.' Dee hugged her parents and Tom shook her dad's hand.

'I'll let them know you want first offer in December when it comes up again,' Tom said cheerfully.

'It will be great to have you up the road Shirley, you can teach me more handiwork,' Julia added.

'I might take your offer up of learning woodturning, Roy,' Patrick joined in.

'What a happy unit we will all be,' Dee reflected.

'And me,' Abbie moved to Dee and tugged on her shirt.

'Yes, you're our Sunday treat Abbie. Talking about sweets what pudding do you want?'

The week that followed seemed a bit of a blur. The house was now decorated, and the garden weeded now that Dee was not working. She spent up to an hour a day in the garden. Often Julia was out there with the twins and life seemed almost idyllic. They just needed the news about Abbie now.

Towards the end of the week, Kate phoned and asked Dee over. When Dee visited it was mid-morning. Kate answered the door still in her nightclothes. Ben had taken Jade out for a walk, so they had an hour together.

'It's my sleep, I just can't get any and I feel shattered. I'm still really sore as well.'

'Are you taking it in turns at night?'

'Yeah, Ben's really good. He says he will do it all, but then I feel bad and useless. He can't win really. I'm just being a cow to him at the minute.'

'Here's our gift,' Dee passed over a lovingly wrapped present.

'Thanks Dee and here's our gift to you, congratulations. We saw it on Facebook.'

Dee spent a lot of time reassuring Kate that it was normal to have the baby blues.

Ben reappeared with Jade who was crying. She needed a feed. Kate took her and attempted to feed her, but Jade was messing about and still crying incessantly. Kate thrust her back to Ben, burst out crying and fled the room.

'This is how she is all the time Dee, I'm really worried and I have to go back to work in a week.'

After reassuring them both that baby blues were quite common Dee left. She sensed that Kate needed a lie down and a sleep.

In the following days Kate dreaded Ben going back to work. She positively begged him not to go, but he had already delayed an important two-day conference. So, he had got to go away for two days. Kate reached out and rang Dee.

'Dee, I'm ringing to ask if you would come and stay with me for a couple of days? Ben's got to go away, and I'm worried about being on my own just yet.'

'Course I will. Don't worry,' Dee said half looking

forward to spending time with a new-born baby and half worried about what Tom would say.

The following Monday, when Dee arrived, she observed that Kate held Jade tenderly although she often got irritated when Jade cried or demanded attention. It was as if, well as if baby Jade was an inconvenience. Kate took little pleasure in any of their normal chat. She concentrated on talking about the trauma of the birth.

'Kate, I know you have me to talk to, but do you think you ought to see the doctor about talking to someone about your feelings at the minute? You can talk about the birth and your sleep and'

'What are you trying to say Dee, that I'm mad or something?' Kate reacted sharply.

'No, of course not but you were saying you feel flat and'

Dee had been here before with Mel. When Mel had children; she had always felt overwhelmed and miserable in the first few weeks. She felt even more worried about Kate though. There was just something she could not put her finger on...

The day after Ben had returned he texted that Kate had had what he described a breakdown in the night, and he was off work with Jade. They were waiting for a mental health nurse to come to see Kate. It turned out that in the night Kate had felt like she wanted to shake Jade to stop her crying and she had confessed this to Ben. Ben had phoned the GP.

Tom and Dee visited that night to see if there was anything they could offer to do. Ben looked at his wits-end. Apparently, Kate had been diagnosed with probable post-natal depression and was going to start anti - depressants. She had now taken to her bed, deciding she needed a complete break from Jade for a couple of days.

'The thing is she is just resting most of the time anyway. Look at the state of the house. She just says she can't do it cause she's tired.' Ben sat with his head in his hands. He explained his boss had not been very understanding about more time off but, more than that, he was worrying about whether Kate was safe with Jade.

'If you trust us to, we'll take Jade to ours till Saturday,' Tom offered. 'Give Kate some complete rest and allow you to go to work Ben.'

'I don't know what to say, I just can't believe this is happening. Kate was looking forward to having the baby.'

'Things will be alright Ben. The anti-depressants will start to work and she's getting counselling daily at the minute you said. Come on get everything together we'll need, check it out with Kate though first.'

They drove back to the cottage, still in a daze at the responsibility they had taken on. Tom planned to arrange some emergency leave.

It turned out it was the best few days they had ever experienced. They sat cuddling, feeding, tickling, bathing, and walking baby Jade. They took her out to see Dee's parents and walked her round to the park. When the Saturday morning came, they didn't want to give her back. They had relished every minute. They had worked well as a team. Tom had done the last feed at midnight while Dee had already got a couple of hours sleep, then Dee did the next feed at three and so forth.

Kate had been missing Jade and had started to ask for her back after the first day, but the nurse and Ben persuaded her to stick to the plan. Kate was now starting to practice mindfulness daily; she had also gone to get her hair cut and this had cheered her. With the help of her nurse, she was going to be doing some self-esteem building and work on processing the trauma she had gone through. The couple had also done some problem solving and had decided to employ a maternity nurse to do sleep -ins to do the night feeds for a month or so. In the day Kate would start to go to mother and baby groups so she did not feel so isolated. There was also a helpline she could ring day or night as well.

On the Saturday, Kate had answered the door to Tom and Dee and took Jade and cuddled her. She smiled.

'Thanks both, for your support, we really appreciate it. I think things will be alright now' and she told them the plans. Ben sat next to her looking lovingly at her, he was hopeful that with all the extra support Kate would become old Kate again.

Dee followed Kate into the kitchen to help do drinks.

'Oh Kate, how are you really?'

'I'm still feeling worried I'm going to be useless as a

mum. I keep trying to think positively though now I have got a mental health nurse and the maternity nurse starts on Monday. It's just been so overwhelming.'

'I know Kate and I'm glad you're accepting the help.'

'I do love her. It is just hard work.'

'Your body will heal, and she'll get into more of a routine with her sleep,' Dee reassured her.

'Ben's so much better with her than me, I'm sure she knows how I'm feeling.'

'Well he's not with her as much as you, it's tiring isn't it when you are with her day and night.'

'Yeah, I know. You must think of me as a terrible person Dee wanting to shake her?'

'No, I just think you are stressed at the minute,' Dee smiled as she took the tray off her.

'Thanks Dee, you're a good friend.'

When Tom and Dee left, they were feeling more confident that Kate would be able to cope. They now needed to focus on their own life.

That Saturday, Dee's dad had gone to have his prostate scan. He had recently been diagnosed with the cancer after having had symptoms and ignoring them for a long time. The scan was to determine the stage of it. As he and Shirley drove home, they were both deep in their own thoughts.

Roy was unsure whether he could stomach any treatment if it were offered and was worrying about how financially secure Shirley would potentially be without him.

Shirley was worried about her husband's health, the prospect of being left alone and more importantly than any of that how would Dee take it?

'Roy when are we going to tell Dee?'

'Not yet Shirl, she's just got engaged and with the fostering and everything. Let us see what we're dealing with first.'

'I'm sure you'll be okay Roy.'

'Yeah course, something else will get me before that does.'

Mog curled up in his basket, he now slept in the kitchen area away from the fire that was rarely on now. As usual he stirred around the same time every night, as the orbs dazzled around him. He missed Tom's mum.

The rest of July and August seemed to go in a flash. There were gardening days, meet up with friends and family days and much communication between the fostering team and themselves. Further information and further fact finding about them as a couple. Then out of the blue on the last week of August they received a phone call from Yvette from the agency. She wanted to come the next day.

‘Well, I guess this is judgement day,’ Tom turned to Dee.

‘Oh Tom, I feel nervous. What if we are rejected and what if we are accepted? Either way our lives will change and well just that I feel nervous,’ Dee sat down gulping a cup of tea.

‘A whole new life for us Dee if we get accepted. The start of our family. Next year we’ll get married and how about trying for a baby then?’

‘Tom, things just don’t seem real. Do they to you?’

‘Yep, real and exciting. Are you going to phone your mum and dad?’

Chapter 44

The next day Yvette arrived. She smiled warmly as they opened the door. 'I've come with good news. Congratulations you have been accepted as foster parents to Abbie.' Tom grabbed hold of Dee's hands and Dee cried. 'Now, can I suggest you move her in at the weekend ready to start her school on Tuesday. Would that be alright with you?'

Back at Abbie's foster home the foster parent was telling Abbie the news. The little girl was so excited and danced around the lounge holding her doll.

'When am I going? Can I go today?'

Once Yvette had gone, Dee rushed to phone her parents. She told them to put the phone on loudspeaker.

'I'm ringing with good news. We've got Abbie.' There was much jubilation by her parents.

Tom and Dee then knocked excitedly on Julia's door.

'I don't know why you doubted it. Congratulations.

This Sunday tea, we'll have a welcome party, round mine if you don't mind me organizing it?'

'Thanks Julia, it will give us time to unpack her on Saturday and everything. That's really kind of you.'

That night Dee drove round to see Claire, she was due to travel to Syria the following week.

'That's fantastic Dee, I'm so pleased I got chance to hear the news before I went.'

Dee started to well up. 'I don't want you to go Claire. I will miss you terribly and I'll worry about you.'

'I'll be back in a few months probably and I'll be able to Facetime you and everything,' Claire said in a reassuring tone.

The two friends hugged, both quietly thinking how much they meant to each other.

'Now I've just got to find Mr. Right. Are you sure Tom hasn't got a brother?' Claire tried to rally round. She explained how her mother was now tentatively back in her life more. Claire had also had some success helping Karis sort through her differences with her dad. It had given Claire something to distract herself from thinking about her own issues. Claire liked to think she was leaving the country on better terms, well, just in case anything bad was going to happen to her or to her family while she was away.

On the drive back from Claire's, Dee stopped outside

her old secondary school. There were so many unhappy memories of been left out, of feeling lonely and different. She had a flashback of walking out of the gate with Mel, giggling and talking about music. Life was certainly more straightforward back then and now look what had happened. She chuckled and said to herself. 'Forget the past, look what I've got to look forward to.'

She took a glimpse at the house opposite the school. In mathematics lessons she used to look at the house and think one day she would like to live there. It looked like a home. She said out loud. 'I've got the home I want, the man I want and now the child I want.'

She smiled to herself and phoned Mel on hands free.

'Guess where I'm sitting?' the two friends spoke about old times and Mel congratulated her on Abbie and reassured her that any time of night or day she could phone her for advice.

'You see Dee, things have worked out for us in the end, haven't they?' Mel reflected.

'Yeah, we've gone through some tough times together Mel but for now things feel good again.'

By the time she got home it was gone ten and Tom was still up. He had started to think about how his life would change. The idea of coming home to Dee and Abbie, his responsibilities and hopes for the wedding. He had also been sitting feeling sad that his parents hadn't been there to share his success. When Dee arrived home, she could tell he had been crying.

‘Hey, you, I didn’t think you’d still be up?’ she snuggled up to Tom on the sofa.

‘He said, ‘I was just thinking about all the good things we’ve got to look forward to and how I wish my parents were still here.’

‘I wish they were as well; they would be really proud of you Tom. You’re an estates manager, you’re a good egg and now you’re going to be a good dad.’

‘I love you, Dee.’

‘I love you, Tom.’

Saturday morning came. An excited Abbie jumped out the car and ran up the path. Tom and Dee were waiting outside with balloons. Tom swirled her up into his arms, then Abbie ran around the house and climbed the stairs and jumped on her bed.

‘Is this my room?’ she gazed at the décor and toys that Dee and Tom had provided for her. She picked things up and played with them while her clothes and possessions were unloaded. Dee and her mum had been out buying a whole new wardrobe of clothes for her as well.

‘Can I call you Mum and Dad? There, straight out of the blue, the words Dee and Tom had longed to hear.

‘Yep, if you want to, we would like that,’ Tom knelt next to her and touched her hand.

The first night was a nightmare in so many ways. Abbie didn't want to go to bed first off, then she wanted Dee and Tom to read her a story in the bed and then she wanted Dee to lie with her to get to sleep. As soon as Dee crept out, she woke again. Then in the middle of the night she crept through into their room and wanted to get into bed with them. Then she was wide awake at six. Tom and Dee were exhausted but at the same time content.

While Dee helped Abbie in the shower, Tom got up and made them all pancakes with syrup. They knew this was Abbie's favourite. Mog stirred in the dining area and allowed Abbie to stroke him. She could be gentle at times; he just was not keen on her trying to pick him up. Then it was out in the garden to explore it and to play ball. By the time four o clock came Dee's parents arrived. They bought a huge present for Abbie - the doll she had wanted.

'Yippee,' Abbie danced around the room with it.

'Come on then, we had better get round to Julia's,' Dee ushered everyone to the door. It was a lovely afternoon, the sun still glowing warm. Julia had set up a tea table in the garden and Patrick had prepared a barbecue. There were welcome banners in the trees. The twins were eagerly running to catch balloons. Julia had hung bunting and fairy lights around the place. It was a magical scene.

'Oh Julia, you have gone to so much trouble thank you so much,' Dee hugged her.

'No, thank you so much for having Abbie and saving me and Patrick from a lifetime of guilt for not having her ourselves. She is a lucky little girl. A real fostering success story, keeping siblings close,' she reflected, at the same time as getting the twins seated with a plate of cheese sandwiches and chocolate fingers.

Dee's parents sat admiring the scene. Dee's dad was, for a couple of hours, a contented man. His daughter had got the life he had wanted for her since the day he held her in his arms for the first time. His wife had found a new role as a nanna and found a new friend in Julia. At Christmas she would have a new house to decorate and faff around in. No, life was not too bad. He just needed the scan to say that the cancer had not spread and was treatable.

'Mum, I'm so happy and when you and dad move here isn't it just going to be perfect,' Dee talked like a small child herself she was so excited.

'Yes darling, it will be perfect. We're so happy for you, at last we can say it and mean it.' As the two women hugged each other, Shirley tried not to cry. She nearly told her daughter the news about her dad, for a minute it felt the right time to do so but she managed to reign herself in.

The following week was utterly chaotic. Dee had to negotiate the school run and their timings needed to be spot on. There were lists on every cupboard door. PE kit days, reading book days, spelling days; play dates. When Abbie was going to bed at eight, so were Dee and Tom. They were both emotionally and physically exhausted.

Chapter 45

Claire and Karis strapped themselves into their seats on the plane for their new life in Syria. As Claire looked out the window and admired the white fluffy clouds, she thought to herself good riddance to the past. 'This is me now, this is just where I want to be. I have made it. I am a good enough person.'

Up in Northumberland, Mel and Mark were strategically planning how to break the news of their engagement over the New Year holiday. Mark had arranged a babysitter one night and had driven Mel to a hidden beauty spot equipped with a picnic basket and a bottle of champagne. He proposed to Mel on the beach and then they lay on the rug eating strawberries and cream. They expected gossip, after all it would have only been a few months since Mel had lost her husband; but they were eager to get on with their lives together and plan a wedding. They had already decided if they were socially castigated, they would look for new ventures, maybe even abroad. Mark was so intent on having a child of his own so that all the children could grow up at a similar age.

Mel looked out to sea and wondered for a moment, just for a second, as to whether she were doing the right thing this time. He was another older man, another knight in shining armour, but this time she somehow felt she was the part of the story that had changed. Going through what she endured with Geoff had made her different inside, stronger. She was no longer a victim in life. If Mark did not live up to what she expected, holy or not, he would be out.

With the help of Liz, the maternity nurse, Kate was beginning to adjust to the demands of motherhood. Her body had recovered, and her mind had caught up with reality. In fact, she was beginning to enjoy parts of it, including showing Jade off in all the new baby clothes and making new friends at the mother and baby class. She was beginning to fall in love with Ben over again and appreciate that although she was not naturally a yummy mummy, she could grow into one. On the off days, she could fake it. Everyone knew celebrities did that.

Chapter 46

While the young around them were making new happier times for themselves, Roy and Shirley's life was getting harder. The scan revealed bad news and there was little chance of a happy ending. They cocooned themselves in, by telling Dee they were full of cold when she phoned. Eventually though Roy sensed it was the right time to tell his news.

Dee's autumn had been taken up in plans for Christmas. Now she was full of guilt that she had not spotted her dad was ill sooner. She was sad that he wasn't going to be a part of Abbie's future for long. Practicality took over and when the rented house came up sooner rather than later, Roy and Shirley moved for their new short time together in the country. Roy managed to enjoy his new man-shed and often sat in there dozing while reading the paper. His woodworking days were gone. Shirley spent most of her time flitting between Roy, Dee and Julia. Carving out a life as the devoted nanna.

Christmas was special, they all pulled together to make it so. Tom invested in a snow machine and dressed up as Santa. They all took Abbie to a Winter Wonderland at the local ski centre and on Christmas day they had tea with Julia.

After the tea was over and they all sat round the table feeling exhausted. Tom cleared his throat and said proudly, 'Dee and I are expecting a baby.'

Glasses were raised to toast the happy news. Roy wanted to speak. 'I just wanted to say how proud we have always been of you Dee. We have always been proud of your achievements at school at work and now how things have turned out for you, Tom and Abbie. We love you all very much. Dee, you have always been beautiful inside and out and now I hope you can see that for yourself.'

Printed in Great Britain
by Amazon

11684619R00164